Mabel Parker

Mabel Parker;
or,
The Hidden Treasure.
A Tale of the Frontier Settlements.

By Horatio Alger, Jr.

With a Preface by Gary Scharnhorst

Archon Books

1986

© 1986 by Gary Scharnhorst
All rights reserved
First published 1986 as an Archon Book,
an imprint of The Shoe String Press, Inc.,
Hamden Connecticut 06514

Printed in the United States of America

The paper in this book
meets the guidelines for performance and durability
of the Committee on Production Guidelines for Book Longevity
of the Council on Library Resources

First Edition

Set in Bembo by
Coghill Composition Co., Richmond, Virginia.

Designed by Jill Breitbarth

Library of Congress Cataloging-in-Publication Data

Alger, Horatio, 1832–1899.
Mabel Parker; or, The hidden treasure.

I. Scharnhorst, Gary. II. Title.
PS1029.A3M33   1986   813'.4   86-3346
ISBN 0-208-02126-4

Preface

"When I began to write for publication," Horatio Alger, Jr., recalled at the end of his long career, "it was far from my expectation that I should devote my life to writing stories for boys. I was ambitious, rather, to write for adults."[1] Though Alger penned a total of 103 juvenile books between 1864 and 1897, he always aspired to literary respectability as an author of adult fiction. Though a prolific writer for boys, he occasionally tried his hand at adult sentimental romance throughout his career.

Predictably, his boudoir tales scarcely qualify as lost or forgotten classics. If they cannot be commended for reasons of literary merit, however, they still warrant modern review. Like antique curios, Alger's adult stories typify a baroque style which has since fallen from fashion. More importantly, Alger varied the themes he routinely developed in his books for boys when he turned to writing fiction for adults. Whereas in his juvenile formula he labored under an obligation to improve his hero's station in the final chapter as a sign of his virtue, in his adult stories he simply arranged for a worthy suitor to woo and wed a genteel heroine. In other words, Alger's adult fiction corrects the popular, albeit mistaken, notion that the author was an unqualified proponent of business success. Alger wrote fables, for both juvenile and adult readers, in which the heroes are invariably rewarded with good fortune, though not necessarily with wealth.[2]

During the 1870s Alger was especially intent on broadening his audience to include adult readers, even while continuing to write two or three juvenile novels per year. In the early 1870s he collaborated with his cousin, William Rounseville Alger, on the official biography of the American actor Edwin Forrest.[3] In 1876, he published a collection of his Civil War ballads and other lyrics to modestly favorable notices in such periodicals as the *Boston Transcript*, the Boston *Literary World*, and the New York *Nation*.[4] In 1877, he published without signature an adult romance entitled *The New Schoolma'am; or, A Summer in North Sparta*. He had written his friend Edwin R. A. Seligman that he would "probably write one novel a year" if this book was a success.[5] When a reviewer for the London *Academy* praised the work as "a sparkling American tale, full of humor,"[6] Alger had every reason to be encouraged. He wrote Seligman that "I am quite ready to believe . . . that there is no higher critical authority in England than the Academy."[7] At the age of forty-five, Alger was poised to abandon the field of juvenile fiction and begin a new career as a writer of local-color and historical fiction for adults.

By July 1878, Alger reported to Seligman that, right on schedule, he had "completed a new novel, nearly half as long again as the 'New Schoolma'am.' " Unfortunately, he added, "I am not sure that it will be published this year. The book-trade is dull, and I prefer to delay it, rather than have it a comparative failure. I shall leave the decision to the publisher."[8] Thus the manuscript of this adult novel, *Mabel Parker; or, The Hidden Treasure*, was laid aside. Just as Alger teetered on the brink of literary respectability, the book-market soured and frustrated his ambitions. He had hoped *Mabel Parker* would earn him accolades. Instead, his publisher at the time, A. K. Loring of Boston, declared bankruptcy in 1881 with the novel still in manuscript. The author subsequently submitted the story to new publishers, Street and Smith of New York, who, to judge from insertions in the manuscript, for a time considered serializing it in seven parts in the old *New York Weekly*. The story has never appeared in its original form until now, however, though Edward Stratemeyer, the creator of the Rover Boys and Tom Swift series, published a version of it rewritten for juvenile readers under the title *Jerry the Backwoods Boy* in 1904. The 203–page manuscript, in Alger's own handwriting with revisions by Stratemeyer, was utterly forgotten until it was unearthed a few years ago in the Street and Smith Collection of the George P. Arents Research Library at Syracuse University.

The novel, with its variation on the popular seduction theme, is hardly distinguishable from other sentimental romances of the period. It contains an Alger boy-hero, a swarthy lad named Zack, but in a subordinate role. The central conflict pits the villainous lawyer Dick Clarke, who tries to extort from Squire Parker permission to wed his beautiful daughter Mabel, against the handsome Henry Davenport, a genteel aristocrat with honorable intentions who has graduated from Harvard College, Alger's own alma mater. A "selfish as well as a proud man," the squire is tempted to accede to Clarke's demand when he is promised the recovery of the lost half of his inheritance, some fifty thousand dollars in gold. A prodigal son, the squire has squandered the other half of his wealth in riotous living. Fortunately, his sins have not been visited upon his pretty and refined daughter. The novel also contains a subplot: In the Indian village near the settlement where the Parkers reside, another love triangle is resolved when a malevolent, stereotypically drunken Indian who wishes to wed the chief's daughter is expelled from the tribe. As a result, the brave Okanoga wins the hand of the beautiful squaw Waurega. The resolution of this subplot anticipates the resolution of the main one. In an encounter of unworthy suitors in the forest, the Indian steals Clarke's purse, a plot contrivance which eventually enables the squire to recover his lost inheritance and the gallant hero to marry his daughter.

Despite its creaky machinations, the tale serves to illustrate how Alger, rather than sanctioning the crass accumulation of wealth, favored the prior claims of domestic harmony, marital bliss, and the moral uses of money. Like a snob from one of Alger's juveniles who has grown to adulthood, Squire Parker receives his inheritance and lives a life of unmerited leisure. His daughter also becomes rich, deservingly so according to the determinism that steadfastly governs the lives of the virtuous in Alger's fiction, but she scorns wealth as if it were a test of her disinterested love. Indeed, she carefully distinguishes between the conditions of wealth and happiness. As she tells her father, "I care not for money. To me it is of no value compared with the happiness which I shall enjoy as Henry's wife." Even the villain Clarke has "the good taste to value youth and beauty above the mere dross of gold," else he would have kept the missing treasure for himself.

Like the sympathetic characters in his other adult fiction, the hero and heroine in this domestic melodrama cherish not wealth but hearth and home. This novel is remarkable, however, for its ambiguous moral and economic implications. Henry and Mabel are genteel by birth, but so are Squire Parker and his smarmy New York friends. The tale is so unlike a conventional success story that the villain is the only character who wishes to rise in rank, a detestable squire the only character who covets money. To his discredit, Dick Clarke considers marriage not a sacrament but a type of "business transaction" and his prospective father-in-law a mere "man of business." Parker's undeserved wealth suggests, as Alger would explicitly indicate in a juvenile novel, that "the evil are sometimes prospered" in this world.[9] Moreover, Clarke's attempt to extort permission to marry Mabel is paralleled, though on a lower frequency, by young Zack's successful extortions of breakfast from Mehitable in chapter VIII and money from Henry Davenport in chapters VII and XVII. Indeed, the troubling similarities between Zack and Dick Clarke are reinforced when, at the end of the novel, the boy-hero becomes a lawyer like the villain.

Perhaps the most salient feature of this "tale of the frontier settlements" is its thinly disguised similarity to *The Pioneers*, the first of James Fenimore Cooper's Leatherstocking tales. Alger's admiration for Cooper's works is well-documented. In his earliest extant letter, written in 1850 while a student at Harvard, he expressed to Cooper "the gratification with which I have perused many of your works—more especially the Leatherstocking series."[10] In later years, Alger often introduced incidents or characters from the Leatherstocking tales in his juvenile novels. For example, he explicitly acknowledged his debt to Cooper for characterizations of savage and noble Indians in *Julius; or, The Street Boy Out West* (1874). He recreated the memorable buffalo stampede described in chapter 19 of *The Prairie* in his novel *The Young Adventurer* (1878), written a few months before *Mabel Parker*. Similarly, he recreated the setting of *The Pioneers*, the lake region of upstate New York around 1820, in *Mabel Parker*. He used the characters of Edward Effingham and Elizabeth Temple, the hero and heroine of Cooper's romance, as models for Henry and Mabel. Alger's debt to Cooper even extended to specific incidents in *Mabel Parker*: The opening chapter of *The Pioneers*, in which two characters argue over rights to a deer both have shot, obviously inspired a similar scene in this novel.

Alger also subscribed, so far as he was able, to the western mythology which Cooper had serviced in the Leatherstocking tales. He actually knew very little, it seems, about the American West. He had spent five months in California the year before he wrote *Mabel Parker*, but he relied almost exclusively on such published sources as the *Pacific Coast Mining Review* and Barry and Patten's *Men and Memories of San Francisco in the Spring of 1850* for the local color and factual details of his western stories.[11] The chapters in *Mabel Parker* set in the Indian village of Okommakamesit are more a temperance tract than an account of authentic Indian customs. Alger expressed his regrets at the beginning of chapter XII that in the preparation of this part of his tale he had consulted Indian chronicles of a "defective character." He was so ignorant or uninventive that at the close of chapter XIII he simply "left to the imagination of the reader" most of the details of Waurega's native dress. Incredibly, he implied in chapter XV that the Indians of a village in upstate New York had once warred with the Seminoles, a tribe indigenous to the southeastern corner of North America.

Notwithstanding his clumsy handling of this material, Alger tapped in the novel the wellsprings of popular attitudes toward the West, in this sense less a place than a symbol. As the opening paragraphs indicate, he has set his tale on the frontier, on the leading edge of civilization at the moment the land is transformed from wilderness to cultivated garden. Alger has dramatized, however banally, the central themes in western American literature: the irresistible progress of white settlers across the continent, the inevitable displacement of the native American tribes. These themes are reduced to their lowest denominator in the final paragraph of the novel, in which Alger explained that "the ruthless march of European civilization" has forced the Indian tribe "beyond the Mississippi" and that "a factory stands on the former site of Long Arrow's lodge." Yet the Indians are not the only misplaced residents of Alger's frontier. Much as the Indians are forced to migrate westward in order to preserve their way of life, Squire Parker epitomizes the artificial eastern aristocracy of birth and wealth which, ill-suited to rugged life in the wilderness, wastes away when thrown upon its own resources. Appropriately enough, he is introduced to the reader as he yearns for his old life in the city while sitting in the easternmost room of his remodeled log cabin.

With surprising subtlety, Squire Parker's daughter mediates between these two extremes in the manner of the classic western hero. She literally incarnates the contradiction of wilderness and civilization which contend on the frontier. "I have no desire to leave the country home which I have found so attractive," she announces at one point in the story. "I was never so happy in the city as I have been here." Mabel is recurrently associated with flowers, especially with wild roses, which may suggest both her beauty and her affinity for natural surroundings. Even Dick Clarke understands that the country is "the fit abiding place of the flowers—more especially of the rose, the queen of flowers." Neither Indian nor effete snob, Mabel Parker is a natural aristocrat of talent and virtue who, like Cooper's Elizabeth Temple or Owen Wister's Molly Wood, is at home on the frontier. Of course, her association with roses may also suggest her latent sexuality. Mabel is introduced to the reader in chapter VII as her lover bids fair to deflower her. Deliberately or not, Alger underscored the unspoken eroticism of their relationship later in the same chapter when Henry confesses his love to Mabel as they sit beneath a phallus-shaped "old tree of huge proportions—a perfect Titan among forest trees." Who would have suspected Alger could treat sexual themes so provocatively?

To reiterate: *Mabel Parker; or, The Hidden Treasure* is no lost lode of literary gold. But neither is it adulterated pulp. Alger exhibited a keen wit in the story, for example, by giving the villainous lawyer and squire the surnames of James Freeman Clarke and Theodore Parker, theological rivals within the old American Unitarian Association of the 1850s. Educated for the Unitarian ministry at the Harvard Divinity School in the late 1850s, Alger seems in the novel to have wished a plague on both their houses. He was especially incensed by Clarke, apparently, for explicitly condemning the "endless reams" of "drivel poured forth by Horatio Alger, Jr." at ceremonies opening a branch of the Boston Public Library in December 1877,[12] about the same time he began to write the novel. So read it for pleasure if you can, collect it as a curiosity if you must. For better or worse, the last Alger novel has taken over a century finally to reach an audience.

I wish to thank Louisa Alger of Cambridge, Massachusetts, for granting me literary rights to this novel. I also wish to thank Paul H. Bonner, Jr., and William P. Rayner of the Condé Nast Publications, which owns the manuscript, for granting me permission to publish it. For the record, I have silently modernized some of Alger's spelling and punctuation, even while resisting the temptation to revise the manuscript more thoroughly. I have also bracketed minor changes in the text where necessary for syntactical or other reasons.

1. "Writing Stories for Boys," *The Writer* 9 (February 1896), 36–37.
2. Gary Scharnhorst, "The Boudoir Tales of Horatio Alger, Jr.," *Journal of Popular Culture* 10 (Summer 1976), 215–226.
3. Scharnhorst, "A Note on the Authorship of Alger's *Life of Edwin Forrest*," *Theatre Studies* 23 (1976–77), 53–55.
4. Scharnhorst and Jack Bales, *Horatio Alger, Jr.: An Annotated Bibliography of Comment and Criticism* (Methuen, New Jersey, and London: Scarecrow, 1981), 34–35.
5. Alger to E. R. A. Seligman, 6 August 1877, Seligman Papers, Butler Library, Columbia University.
6. London *Academy*, 15 December 1877, 548.
7. Alger to E. R. A. Seligman, 3 January 1878, Seligman Papers, Butler Library, Columbia University.
8. Alger to E. R. A. Seligman, 15 July 1878, Seligman Papers, Butler Library, Columbia University.
9. *A Cousin's Conspiracy* (New York: New York Book Co., 1909), 12.
10. Alger to James Fenimore Cooper, 12 September 1850, Beinecke Library, Yale University. See also Scharnhorst, "Had Their Mothers Only Known: Horatio Alger, Jr., Rewrites Cooper, Melville, and Twain," *Journal of American Culture* 5 (Summer 1982), 91–95.
11. Scharnhorst with Jack Bales, *The Lost Life of Horatio Alger, Jr.* (Bloomington: Indiana University Press, 1985), 114.
12. "Literary Rubbish," *Library Journal* 2 (January–February 1878), 299.

Gary Scharnhorst
University of Texas at Dallas

Chapter I.

Night in the Woods.

Sixty years since, a large part of central and western New York was a wilderness in which civilization had only gained an occasional foothold. Even Buffalo, now a great, bustling city numbering hard upon a hundred thousand inhabitants, was, at that time, a small village containing but a few hundreds. East and west have proved strangely relative terms, and our western frontier has been steadily advancing towards the Pacific coast. But frontier life today has a very different meaning from frontier life fifty years since. The appliances of a refined social life have found their way beyond the Mississippi, and, judging from the past, it would scarcely be surprising if, not many years hence, flourishing villages should spring up in the shadow of the Rocky Mountains.

Some of the pleasantest portions of the Empire state were and still are to be found in the neighborhood of those beautiful lakes which cluster together in central New York. At the time that my story opens, settlements here were few and far between, and the aboriginal inhabitants had not wholly deserted the rich hunting grounds through which they once roamed undisturbed. Where may now be seen open fields highly cultivated, lingered untouched large sections of the primitive forest, destined eventually to fall before the axe of the settler.

Night was rapidly settling down upon the landscape, when a horseman might have been seen guiding his horse with an air of anxious uncertainty along a bridle path, which, in the obscurity, it was somewhat difficult to make out. It is unnecessary to indicate the locality farther than to say that it was but a few miles distant from Lake Canandaigua. The horseman, or rather the pedestrian, for he had dismounted and was now leading his horse, was a stout man ranging in age from forty to fifty. He had a round, bullet head, and sharp ferret-like eyes, which taken in connection with a spreading pug nose and a mottled complexion, could scarcely be said to make an attractive countenance even under the most favorable circumstances.

Now, however, that symptoms of decided ill-humor were plainly to be read in the contracted brow and the scowling eyes, the effect was even more disagreeable.

"A pretty prospect," grumbled the traveller. "Here am I, with nothing to eat since early this morning, wandering at random in this accursed wilderness, with no chance, that I can see, of a resting place. Serves me right for coming out here on what may after all prove a wild goose chase. And yet," he added more thoughtfully, "if I only succeed in my plans, I will not grudge the trouble I have been at. And I shall succeed, I feel sure. There's nothing that Dick Clarke has set himself to accomplish yet that he has failed in. Hark, what is that?"

As he spoke, the dull rumbling of distant thunder came to his ears, and instantly the rain in thick drops began to patter down among the forest leaves.

"There's something more to be thankful for," muttered the traveller with increased peevishness. "It seems as if all the powers of nature were conspiring against me. But if I were only sure of a shelter and a little something to stay my famished stomach, I wouldn't mind. A warm heart and a good conscience I've heard spoken of as good companions, but for my part give me a warm fire and a good belly full, and I'll be content."

Meanwhile, the darkness had rapidly increased, making the task of guiding the horse more difficult than before. Add to this that the beast was terrified by the storm and lightning and half disposed to break away from his guide, and we have a complication of troubles which Dick Clarke was scarcely Christian enough to endure without grumbling.

As he strode on with hesitating steps a foot or two in advance of the horse whom he led by his bridle, he suddenly felt that he had stepped upon a soft substance, the nature of which very speedily made itself manifest by the springing up of a tall Indian in his path.

"Ha! what have we here?" explained Dick, startled. "My good friend, you appear to have singular taste in selecting such a time and such a place for repose."

"All places alike to Logan" was the moody reply.

"Well, they are not to me, by a great sight. I can think of a good many that I should prefer. Can you direct me to any place where I can obtain shelter for the night and something to eat?"

"No—none near" was the reply, and the Indian seemed ready to lie down again, when Dick, feeling that if this resource failed him he should be compelled to remain all night exposed to the inclemency of the weather, said more urgently, "Think a little, my good friend. I know you can call to mind some place, however poor, where I may at least be sheltered from this accursed rain which has completely drenched me. Perhaps this will help your recollection."

As he said these last words he held up a coin, which, in spite of the darkness, the Indian could see, hoping by this to tempt him to that for which he had no inclination.

The bait took, for Logan snatched it from his hand, and before the traveller, startled by the suddenness of the proceeding, had decided whether to construe it into an acceptance of his offer or as an act of pillage, the Indian decided the matter by taking a step forward and saying sententiously, "Me lead, you follow," and walked steadily onward, showing by his freedom from uncertainty not only that he was accustomed to the place but that his sight was keener than that of his companion.

Those are most likely to indulge in suspicions of their

3

fellow men who are least worthy of trust themselves, and Dick Clarke, many parts of whose life would scarcely have borne a very rigid examination, could not help feeling some doubts as to the good intentions of his savage guide.

"Who knows where the fellow is leading me?" thought he. "I may have got myself into a worse scrape even than staying all night exposed to this pouring rain. I couldn't see the fellow's face very distinctly, but he looked rather sullen. And then the way he grabbed the money was a little suspicious. He may be luring me to some place where he can murder me for what gold I may have about me, though, for that matter, I must confess he need not choose a darker or more convenient spot than that where we met. However, it may be as well for me to keep a sharp look out."

So saying, or rather thinking, Dick felt carefully to see that his pistols were in their wonted place, ready to use at a moment's notice, in case the Indian should see fit to act on the offensive.

"I own," soliloquized Dick, "that I should not like to have my scalp dangling from yonder fellow's waist. It's a kind of death that would have more terrors for me than any on the battle field. However, I see we are getting to where the trees are not quite so thick, and I can see a little better."

In fact, the Indian had guided him by a winding path to the skirt of the wood where, although he was more exposed to the force of the storm, it seemed at all events less dismal than in the forest.

Dick Clarke began to feel greater confidence than at first in the fidelity of his guide, and pressed forward to the side of the latter, who was striding before him at a distance of perhaps a rod.

"Where are you going to carry me?" he inquired, looking about him in vain for a light of some kind which should indicate a house.

"To tavern," answered the Indian with laconic brevity.

"Tavern? Indeed I am glad to find that they have any institutions that remind one of civilization. To my mind this

4

is about the wildest country I ever visited. I don't see how anybody can be contented to live hereabouts."

The Indian talked English but little, but could understand better than he could make use of it. At all events, it was probable he comprehended the not over complimentary remark upon his neighborhood from the pointed nature of his reply.

"Why come here, then?" he asked significantly.

"O, as to that," said the other after a moment's pause, "we sometimes have to go where we would rather not. I shouldn't have come here if I hadn't had something to bring me here, you may be sure of that. However, be that as it may, I'm here, and I feel a little interest about knowing when I am likely to find shelter. How far off is this tavern that you propose to guide me to?"

"About three mile," said the Indian as indifferently as if he had not got the distance to traverse as well as his companion.

"Three miles!" exclaimed Dick in dismay. "Well, that's what I call a very pleasant piece of information under the circumstances. It's only to be hoped that when I get there I shall be repaid for the trouble I have taken in travelling to it. But, as we have got into a comparatively open path, I might as well mount the sorrel here, who, I am inclined to think, will be as glad to find shelter as I am."

The rest of the journey passed in silence. The Indian was reticent by nature and Dick Clarke was occupied by thoughts of his own.

Chapter II.

Hill's Tavern.

Probably neither the Indian nor his companion were sorry to come in sight of the building which was known for twenty miles around as "Hill's Tavern."

It was not a large building, and the accommodations which it could offer travellers must have been very limited. But its chief business was not that of providing lodgings. Travellers were too few in number to make that a very important item in the business carried on. The bar was decidedly the leading feature of the establishment, and the amount of liquor consumed in the rude barroom would have appalled an advocate of temperance. It was not unusual, when the evenings were pleasant, to find a majority of the settlers living within five miles gathered in the barroom alternately drinking and gossiping. Nor was the patronage confined to whites. Here, as elsewhere, one of the earliest lessons in civilization for which the Indians were indebted to their white brethren was the taste for rum, or "firewater" as they not inappropriately designated it, and a large share of the proceeds of Indian industry, whenever they could be induced to work, went for intoxicating drinks.

On this particular evening, the fury of the elements had prevented the usual collection in the barroom. The landlord had not opened the door for a single customer through the evening, and he had about decided to close for the night when a knock was heard at the door.

Pricking up his ears with professional eagerness, the portly landlord (who rejoiced in the military designation of

Captain Hill) hastened to the door which he had already fastened, and, withdrawing the bolt, looked out to see who his late guests might be.

At first he only caught sight of the Indian who was generally known in the settlement as Jack. With a feeling of disappointment, for the Indian's patronage would hardly be sufficient to make it worth while to forego his purpose, he said, "You're too late, Jack. I am just going to close."

"Hallo there, landlord!" exclaimed Dick Clarke, coming forward in some alarm lest he should, after all, be deprived of the shelter which had cost him so much trouble to reach. "Is it the custom in your neighborhood to shut your doors upon guests that reach you no later than nine o'clock, and in such a storm too? Gad, if it is, I must say it is the most inhospitable region I ever came into, that's all."

"I beg your pardon, sir," said the landlord with deference. "I didn't see you. I thought it was only Jack here, and I knew he might have come in the daytime for the glass of liquor which, I suppose, is all that he is after."

"I must do Jack, if that is his name, the justice to say that he would never have thought of coming at all if I hadn't tried the effect of a little silver upon him. But, being here, I suppose he would not object to a little something hot to make him forget the wet and cold from which he, as well as myself, is suffering."

The Indian, who had been standing by in seeming apathy, seemed to understand the meaning of what had been said, for his eye brightened with eagerness and he ejaculated eagerly, "Yes—yes. Me like rum."

"No doubt about that," commented the landlord, adding, "Don't you think you'd feel better for taking a little yourself, sir?"

"Faith, it's not a bad proposition. I think I'll accept it," said the traveller throwing off his dripping overcoat and taking a seat near the fireplace in which a huge backlog was burning brightly. "I begin to think better of your country, landlord, than I was disposed to do a couple of hours since."

7

"It's a pleasant country, sir,—fine soil."

"I dare say," returned his guest carelessly, "but you'll admit that my reception until now has not been of a nature to make my first impressions very pleasant."

"Then you've never been this way before," said the landlord, indulging a curiosity for which his fraternity are somewhat noted.

"Never in my life before. I didn't know the settlements extended out so far."

"You come, mayhap, from the city of New York?" suggested the landlord in an inquiring tone.

"Mayhap I do" was the not very decisive reply. "At any rate I have been there. It is quite a promising place. A good deal of business done there."

"So I have always heard," returned the landlord. "But, after all, I don't like being cooped up in a city. Give me the country, where I can have plenty of elbow room. However, I might feel differently if I were in a good business in the city. Perhaps you are so engaged, Mr. —— ahem, your name escaped me."

"I don't remember having mentioned it," said Clarke with a little malicious enjoyment in disappointing the landlord's evident desire to find out who he was.

"Ah, indeed, perhaps not," said the portly host, not abashed. "I only thought it would be convenient to know what to call you. I'm thankful to say that I am not one of those landlords that are constantly prying into the business of their guests, and all about them. Are you intending to stay long in this part of the country, sir?"

The inconsistency between the first and the last parts of the landlord's remarks brought a smile to the face of Dick Clarke, who, however, saw fit to cease quizzing his host and communicate at once all that he was intending to do.

"You may call me Clarke," he said. "As to my stay that will be guided entirely by circumstances. Perhaps it is as much curiosity as anything which has brought me here. I have heard of the beauties of your scenery, of which perhaps I have not at present an adequate appreciation. For an idler like myself, I don't know but I may be as well off here as anywhere."

"He is not in business," inferred the landlord. "I dare say he is looking about with the intention of settling down here. I hope he will. He looks like a man of some means and would no doubt contrive to spend a part of it with me. The larger the settlement, the better my chances of my growing rich."

"I trust you will favor my house with your presence, as long as you see fit to remain," he said obsequiously.

"I dare say I shall," said Clarke carelessly. "By the way, how long have you been located here?"

"It is four years since I first set up this tavern, called after me, as you see. At that time there were fewer people in the settlement than now, and my customers were few, but more families have come in since and I am doing pretty well at the present time."

Meanwhile, Dick Clarke drew off his boots and proceeded to dry his wet feet at the fire. Leaning luxuriously back in the rocking chair which he occupied, he turned towards the landlord and asked with the air of one not much interested but who only asked for the sake of keeping up the conversation: "Pray tell me who are some of your chief settlers? It is just possible that I may have met or heard of some of them before."

The landlord, nothing loath to gossip with his guest, commenced: "There's Isaac Davenport,—Major Davenport most people call him. I believe he was an officer in the war. He's about the earliest of our settlers and owns a large tract of land. A fine man, the Major is."

"Any family?" queried Dick Clarke, half closing his eyes.

"Yes, he's got a son—nigh on to twenty-two he must be now. Being the Major's only son he's taken a good deal of pains with him—sent him off to the East to be educated. Let me see, there's a college at Cambridge, isn't there?"

"Yes, Harvard College."

"That's the place. Well, the young man got his schooling there, and a fine scholar he was—at the head of his class I've heard. But he's been back here now about a year and a half.

9

Some say he brought home a lot of law books and is studying law at home, but I don't know for certain about that."

"Who else have you among your principal men?" asked his guest, who apparently took less interest in young Davenport than the narrator.

"There's Squire Parker—"

The traveller started. "What is his first name—his Christian name, I mean?"

"Joseph, I believe. Do you know him?"

"Probably not. I have known a man of that name, but the name is common. I presume you find it everywhere. But go on. Tell me something of this man."

"I don't know very much to tell," answered the landlord. "He lives about five miles from here in a lonely place, and keeps very much to himself, which I think is a pity, not so much on his account, but it must be dull for his daughter, who is as pretty a damsel of eighteen summers as you will be likely to see anywhere about."

"Ah, he has a pretty daughter, then, has he?" said Clarke, veiling under an indifferent manner a stronger feeling of curiosity than he had yet felt.

"That he has, and I rather think there's a certain young gentleman has found it out."

"Ha, has she a suitor?" demanded the traveller with a visible air of chagrin which was somewhat surprising in one who professed to have heard of her for the first time only the moment before.

The landlord, however, was somewhat obtuse, and noticed nothing remarkable in the tone of his guest.

"It's that same young man I was just telling you about," he continued, "Major Davenport's son Henry. I oftentimes see them walking or riding together and I guess Major Davenport's is the only house where Squire Parker goes. As I told you only a minute or two since, he isn't inclined to be very social, and keeps pretty much to himself."

"Does Mabel Parker, think you, encourage the attentions of this young"—jackanapes, the speaker was about to say, but paused on the instant, and substituted "man?"

One point, however, his caution had overlooked. He had unwittingly used the young lady's Christian name. The landlord did not fail to notice this slip and asked with an air of surprise, "You know her then?"

"From what do you infer that?" said Clarke unsuspiciously.

"How should you know that her name was Mabel Parker, otherwise?"

"From your mentioning it, of course, landlord," said Dick Clarke with unblushing assurance. "How else should I know it?"

"I suppose I did name it, then," said the landlord, overborne by the other's confident declaration, "although I don't remember it."

"However, though I don't know her now," continued Clarke, "your representations have so stimulated my curiosity that I shall certainly take the earliest opportunity of making her acquaintance, that is if I remain here long enough."

"They ain't so come-at-able as some," said the landlord dubiously.

"All things are possible to the daring," said Dick lightly. "Perhaps I may yet cut out this college stripling of yours."

"He is a good-looking fellow," said the landlord who had been won, by the young man's frank and affable bearing, to take quite a strong interest in his success. As he said this, it was only natural that he should cast a glance at the not overprepossessing countenance of his guest, who, in addition to the disadvantage of never having been born very handsome, had suffered the wear and tear of at least twice as many years as had passed over the head of the youthful rival.

Dick Clarke penetrated the landlord's meaning with no great difficulty, but it was not one of his foibles to be sensitive on the score of his personal appearance. Accordingly, he said in a good humored way, "And you mean to intimate, friend landlord, that, in that respect, he has the decided advantage of me?"

"I don't deny, sir," said the landlord hastily, not wishing

11

to offend his guest, "that you are a very good-looking man of your years. But you know these girls are apt to fancy young sprigs, rather than fine, mature men like you or me."

Dick Clarke smilingly surveyed his host's proportions and replied: "Perhaps they don't regard personal appearance so much as you think, my good friend. It isn't all that sound a woman's heart or read her preferences. However, it isn't worthwhile to spend too much time upon a girl I have not seen and may not like. I may be very willing to leave her to the young Davenport after all. But I see by your clock in the corner that it is getting late, at any rate for one who has been on a horse's back pretty much all day. I suppose you can furnish me with a comfortable chamber."

"Yes, sir, I can give you a good, comfortable room where I have no doubt you will sleep as sound as a top. But perhaps you will take another glass to serve as a nightcap. It's a sovereign thing to give one a good night's rest."

"I don't care if I do" was the reply, "provided you will join me in it."

"That I will with great pleasure," said Captain Hill, with a heartiness which left no doubt of his sincerity. "I'll drink your health in a bumper."

"And success to my suit, eh, landlord?"

"Yes, provided you don't trespass on another's manor."

"That qualification spoils all. But here's one I warrant will drink without any such qualifications. Do you think you can stand another glass, Jack?"

The Indian came forward from the settle on which he was reclining and expressed his eager assent.

"Jack is always on hand," said the landlord. "If he keeps on drinking at this rate, he'll lose half his name, and become a *demi-john*."

The landlord laughed obstreperously at his own witticism which so far put him in good humor that he gave Jack permission to spend the night on the settle which he had already occupied during a part of the evening.

12

Chapter III.

Squire Parker's Household.

Presuming that the reader may feel desirous of knowing more of the Parkers in whom Dick Clarke appears to take so mysterious an interest, we propose to change the scene from the rude tavern to the dwelling of Squire Parker. It may be mentioned, by the way, that the title "Squire" was a title of courtesy only, being conferred out of deference to the supposed wealth of the bearer.

The site of the dwelling was well-chosen. It crowned the summit of an elevation sloping gradually to a beautiful pond or lakelet which though not large in extent was of considerable depth. Except on the side which looked towards the house, the banks were adorned with sightly trees, some throwing their branches far out over the placid water and so furnishing a refreshing shelter from the fervor of the summer sun. Mabel Parker often floated in a boat kept for her use upon the pond under the shelter of these fine old trees, sometimes in company with young Davenport, who was always ready to proffer his assistance.

Contrary to the usual custom (for the pioneer is not often a man who has an appreciation of the tasteful and beautiful) a few trees had been [left] standing in the neighborhood of the house so that its first appearance, when seen through the leaves of the stately trees which stood before it, was pleasingly rural. For this evidence of taste the present occupant was not entitled to the sole credit, since the clearing had been originally made by another who was induced to sell out in consideration of a handsome advance upon the original cost.

In like manner the nucleus of the present dwelling had been erected by the first settler. It had been but an ordinary log cabin containing two rooms and wholly without architectural ornament. The purchaser, instead of pulling it down and erecting a dwelling more like those in the more settled parts of the country, determined to see what a transformation could be effected by taste in the somewhat unpromising material furnished him. Accordingly, he elevated it to two stories and so enlarged it in the rear as nearly to double its accommodations. On two sides ran a rustic piazza, around the columns of which vines had been taught to clamber. It was a log cabin still, but a log cabin in the highest style of art of which such a building is capable, infinitely preferable, certainly so far as appropriateness went, to the timber palaces which disfigure so many of our New England villages.

Beside the cabin a moderate space was devoted to the culture of flowers, and presented, with its many hues, crimson and golden predominating, a very attractive picture. This was under the especial charge of Mabel Parker, who had brought the seeds with her from the East. Fortunately, she had a more delicate appreciation of such things than the spinster who had accompanied them as handmaiden, though the position which she occupied in the family approximated more nearly, in respect to the freedom it conferred, to the more honorable office of housekeeper.

Mehitable Higgins deserves more than a passing notice at our hands. She was tall, angular, and bony, and to judge from present appearances, could never have possessed a very large share of that beauty which is said to be but skin-deep. Yet such is the liability to self-deception that Mehitable was by no means sensible of her deficiency in personal attractions, but evidently thought herself a handsome woman still, if we may judge from the numerous glances which she cast at the mirror as she passed to and fro before it in her daily round of duty. It would be hard to tell by what magical process the sallow and wrinkled cheek, the long and hooked nose, and the pursed-up mouth were invested with beauty even to the partial gaze of the owner, but perhaps it is a mercy that we cannot, as the poet expresses it, "see ourselves as others see us."

As Mehitable had attained the mature age of forty-seven years without marrying, it was quite doubtful whether she would ever have an opportunity to do so. It was her habit to indulge in mysterious hints respecting a certain Joshua Perkins who, she would have it believed, was madly in love with her at some period in the past, but whom she had disappointed with a flinty refusal. She further hinted,—for on this subject she never came directly to the point but spoke with a degree of circumlocution and indirectness,—that the said Joshua was plunged into such a state of distraction by his disappointment that he made frantic efforts to put an end to his existence and was only deterred therefrom by the united efforts of all his relatives.

There were some uncharitable persons who suspected that Joshua Perkins was a mythical personage and only existed in the excited fancy of Mehitable, but the present historian confesses himself unable to solve the question which is thus started. He is inclined to the opinion, however, that he was a real personage, but that his preference for Mehitable's society, proposal to her, and subsequent state of despair were innocent figments of that lady's imagination.

This myth, or whatever it may be called, saved Mehitable from the more common resource of a spinster, railing against matrimony. She thought she might make up her mind to marry if she should ever meet with a congenial spirit, but all overtures from those who could not be classed as such she was determined sternly to reject. By a kind obliviousness not uncommon, she ignored the passage of time for fifteen years or more, and although her age was forty-seven was accustomed to call herself about thirty.

She was, in her secret heart, jealous of the superior youth and beauty of her young mistress, and was wont to depreciate, as far as she dared, the tastes and employments to which Mabel was partial.

"I don't see the use of giving up so much time to flowers and such trash," she was heard to say more than once. "They ain't good to eat, like cabbages and onions. All they are fit for is to smell of, and a body doesn't want to be smelling all the time."

"Didn't you like flowers when you were young, Hitty?" asked Zack (abbreviated from Zachariah), a boy in Squire Parker's employ, whose great delight it was to provoke Mehitable.

"When I was young!" retorted Mehitable, pausing from her work. "One would think from the way you talk that I was an old woman. I'd have you to know that I'm not so very much older than Mabel."

Zack whistled.

This Mehitable correctly interpreted to indicate incredulity and proceeded: "If you want to whistle, Zack, you'd better go out of the house. It's improper, and impolite. You'd better be out in the field hoeing them turnips instead of idling 'round here."

"Well, I will, Hitty—"

"There's no call for you to address me with such familiarity," interrupted Mehitable in a dignified manner. "My name is Mehitable."

"Well, then, Mehitable, would you be willing to tell me just how old you are?"

"Thank goodness, I ain't ashamed of my age. I'm about thirty."

"O dear!" ejaculated Zack in comic consternation.

"What's the matter now?" demanded Mehitable sharply.

"I was thinking how bad I should feel to look so old when I am thirty."

"Clear out of this room instantly," exclaimed the exasperated spinster, advancing threateningly with the broom.

Of Zack, who has thus been introduced as a pendant to Mehitable, it may be said that he was a bright active boy of thirteen and contributed not a little by his lively disposition to the life of the house. If his fun now and then bordered upon mischief, it was quite impossible to suspect one with such a frank good humored face of harboring malice, and he generally escaped any but the mildest censure. He was employed in chores and light labors about the house, and his education was superintended by Mabel herself, though it must be acknowledged that Zack would have much preferred [to spend] these enforced hours of study [in] hunting birds' nests, setting traps for squirrels, or other boyish amusements. But two hours daily were strictly required of him for study, and it must be admitted in justice that his natural abilities were so good as, when fairly exercised, to advance him rapidly.

It is perhaps hardly rulable to devote so much space to what may properly be regarded as subordinate characters and reserve their superiors for an after description. For this I have no apology to offer, unless that these will be left rather to the general course of the story to evolve. A few words, however, are required by way of introduction.

Squire Parker was tall of stature and, though but little over forty years of age, had begun to stoop somewhat. There were in his face certain indications which would lead one to suspect that his life had been clouded by some circumstance, from the effects of which he had not yet recovered. His temperament was mild and, in speech, he was somewhat sparing of words. There was a contrast between his manner and that of his daughter, who was disposed to be lively and who habitually looked on the bright side of things.

The praises in which the landlord indulged respecting Mabel were deserved. Of medium stature, her figure combined plumpness with perfect grace and ease of movement without approaching that condition of adiposity which Byron apprehended with such alarm. The freedom with which she exercised in the open air had been in the highest degree beneficial to her health and her clear blue eye, and the rich bloom which mantled her cheek evinced nothing of that delicacy and fragility which too often characterize the young ladies of the present day.

Of this meagre description, Mabel must be allowed to fill out the outlines, herself, as the story proceeds.

17

Chapter IV.

Zack's Hunting Adventure.

The morning succeeding the stormy night in which our traveller found a refuge at the tavern was singularly beautiful. The sun was shining brightly. The valleys and meadows were green with waving grass, sprinkled plentifully with cowslips and dandelions. It was one of those mornings on which life itself becomes a luxury and an intoxication.

Upon this morning Zack had pitched for carrying out a plan which he had long been contemplating. It was briefly this. So recent had been the settlement of this part of the country that the shy denizens of the forest—the deer of the Indian hunting grounds—had not yet disappeared. Occasionally, a hunter would bring one into the village, though as the deer thinned out, such occasions became more and more rare and became invested with increased importance.

It was this circumstance, perhaps, that shaped Zack's youthful ambition. He had read unmoved the lives of distinguished writers and judges, but the thought of slaying a deer without assistance from anyone powerfully excited his emulation. He had, now and then, caught a glimpse of a deer dashing rapidly through the forest walks and felt no doubt that if provided with a weapon he could bring one down.

There was a gun kept in an outbuilding, belonging to a man whom Mr. Parker employed during the busy season. When Zack had made up his mind to try his luck as a hunter, it was this weapon which he proposed to use.

On this particular morning, after his duties were over, he took an opportunity when Mehitable was on the other side of the house hanging out clothes to steal into the place where the gun was kept, hastily seize it, and darting forth, [he] made for the woods which were at no great distance from the house.

"Now I'm all ready to pepper 'em," said Zack exultingly. "I wonder what they'll all say at the house if I come home with a fine, fat deer. It'll keep us in dinners for a week."

Leaving Zack to trudge along in the direction of the forest, we return to our first acquaintance at Hill's Tavern.

Mr. Clarke did not arise very early. The fatigue of the previous day had been so great that exhausted Nature required a longer time than usual to recuperate. When he did arouse himself the sun was already high in the heavens.

After two or three preliminary yawns our traveller roused himself and made his morning toilet.

"After all, 'tain't so bad a country," he soliloquized, taking a leisurely survey from the window of the varied scenery that lay stretched out beneath in all the glory of morning sunshine. "I thought last night I should be glad to get away from it—that is when my object is accomplished—but this morning puts quite a different face on the matter. The climate or something else has had a wonderful effect in promoting my appetite. I don't remember when I have been so sharp set. I think I'll go down and see what sort of a breakfast I can get."

On descending to the lower part of the house Mr. Clarke found the table already spread and the breakfast awaiting his attack.

"I heard you stirring 'round upstairs," said the landlord, "and thought I'd have breakfast put on the table. We took ours about two hours ago, but calculated you might be tired and wouldn't disturb you. Hope you had a comfortable sleep."

"Capital, capital, my good host, and it has given me a famous appetite. I have no doubt I shall do ample justice to your breakfast."

The fare provided might well tempt an epicure. However

much the cities of the seaboard might have the advantage in other respects, they could not have furnished a more delicious meal than this rude tavern. The woods contributed wild honey and maple syrup, and these with milk, eggs, hominy and corn bread and the flesh of the wild pheasant furnished forth a meal, upon the dispatch of which the newcomer entered with the greatest zest.

After half an hour busily spent he rose from the table with a sigh of relief, and in that comfortable state which accompanies a full stomach sauntered out to the barroom where he decided to complete his meal with a glass of brandy.

"What do you propose to do with yourself today?" asked the complaisant landlord. "Hope you'll find enough to amuse you so that we can keep you here a good while."

"Perhaps you may, landlord. I certainly like your country very much better this morning than I did last night, and your breakfast has added to the favorable impression. I think I shall go out and reconnoitre a little. I think you mentioned a Mr. Parker last evening."

"Squire Parker."

"Yes, Squire Parker. Whereabouts does he live? In the neighborhood?"

"Some distance off, sir. It must be nearly five miles."

"And in what direction?"

"You see them woods there? Well, it's on the other side of them that the Squire lives."

"Then it would be a saving of distance for one that wanted to go there to go through them?"

"Yes, it would shorten it a good deal. Are you going to see the Squire?"

"I don't know as to that," said the other evasively. "As the country is all new to me I might as well go there as anywhere to look about. Besides, I can't help feeling interested in the daughter after all you've told me."

"Mabel Parker's a hansum gal, that's a fact, and will make a fine wife for young Davenport," said the landlord.

"Not if I can help it," muttered Clarke.

"What did you say, sir?" queried his host.

"Nothing of consequence," said the other hurriedly. "I think I'll try the woods, then, landlord, and perhaps I may seek out this man you speak of."

"Wouldn't you like to take a gun with you, sir? There's a deal of game that maybe you might like a shot at."

"Not this morning," said Dick. "I think I won't trouble you. Some other time perhaps—"

"Jest as you say, Squire. The musket's at your service any time."

Thanking the landlord for his offer, our acquaintance took his way to the forest. It was well-grown, some of the trees having reached an age almost patriarchal. Perhaps if our friend had been a poet or a sentimentalist, he might have experienced something of the pleasure which Byron found in the "pathless woods," but he was not troubled in this way. His mind was a practical one, and its peculiar training—for he had been educated a lawyer—had a tendency to make it more so. He had always lived in a city or large town and had little taste for or appreciation of natural scenery.

As he was making his way through the wood, he was startled by the cry of a stray bird, which suggested to him the possibility of encountering some ill-disposed Indians, which he had heard were wont to be in ambush behind trees.

"It would be decidedly disagreeable," he thought, "if some of the prowling savages, provided there are any, and this wood certainly seems lonely enough for their lurking place, should take it into their heads to make a mark of me."

Scarcely had this thought shaped itself in his mind when, as if prophetic, it was followed by the discharge of a gun, the bullet of which lodged in his hat.

Though perhaps not more timid than the majority of people, it is scarcely a matter of surprise that our hero should have been struck with consternation at this sudden attack, and, conscious that he was wholly unarmed, should have put in force his first instinctive impulse to flee.

But it so happened that the bullet, instead of having been sent from in front, had actually been discharged by someone in his rear,—so that the result of his attempt to escape was to confront him with the perpetrator of the assault, in the shape of our would-be deerslayer, Zack.

When the eyes of Mr. Clarke rested on the boy running up with his gun swung across his two hands, eager probably to take possession of the game, he stopped short in stupefaction.

"Good Heavens!" was his first thought, "what a singular state of society this must be when a boy coolly makes a mark of any stranger he happens to meet. And there the young rascal is staring at me, in disappointment I suppose, to think his shot has not taken effect. What fiend possessed you to shoot at me, boy?" he demanded sternly. "What have I done, that you should seek my life?"

"Seek your life, sir," said Zack vacantly.

"Certainly. Don't you see that bullet-hole? An inch or two lower, and it would have pierced my skull."

"I—I thought you was a deer," faltered Zack, beginning to be terrified for the consequences of his precipitation.

"Thought I was a deer! Do I look like a deer?" demanded the exasperated traveller.

"N'no, sir."

"Then what made you take me for one?"

"I heard you moving, and thought you was a deer."

"You did, eh! Why didn't you wait till you found out, before you thought proper to shoot at me?"

"Because I was afraid if I waited I should miss you—I mean the deer, sir," said Zack, getting more and more confused as his explanation went on.

"That is very satisfactory," returned Dick, still irate. "You preferred the risk of killing me to the risk of losing your deer. Human life must be very cheap in this part of the world. May I inquire, as a simple matter of curiosity, how many men you have shot by mistake for deer during your hunting experience?"

"None, sir. You're the first deer I ever mistook for a

man—I mean the first man I ever mistook for a deer," said Zack, getting more and more mixed up in his speech.

"What should you have done in case you had killed me?"

"I don't know," said Zack helplessly.

"Give me that gun," said Clarke imperatively.

"O, you ain't going to shoot me, are you?" exclaimed Zack, terror overspreading his face and his ruddy color giving place to paleness.

"Isn't it fair," said Clarke, maliciously enjoying the boy's terror, "that I should have a shot at you in return for the one with which you favored me?"

"O don't, sir, don't! I'll never shoot at a deer again in my life."

"How is that going to benefit me? Perhaps you will shoot at me instead."

Zack vehemently protested that he cherished no such bloody intention, and Clarke, to his great relief, did not insist upon the retaliation referred to.

"Where do you live?" inquired Clarke after a pause.

"With Squire Parker, over there."

"Ha! you are not his son? I never heard that he had any."

"No, I only live with him to do chores and such like."

"Then you can direct me to his house."

"You ain't going to tell him about my shooting you?" asked Zack apprehensively.

"I don't know. I haven't made up my mind."

"Then what are you going to see him for?" asked the boy anxiously.

"My boy, I advise you not to be too inquisitive. I may have other matters to confer with him about besides this affair of yours. Conduct me as quickly as possible to his house, and I will take into consideration the expediency of informing him of your assault upon me."

"I hope Mehitable won't hear of it," thought Zack, as he silently proceeded to obey Clarke's request. "She wouldn't let me rest, night or day. Darned if it's such fun deer hunting as I thought."

"This is certainly a promising commencement of my

adventures," reflected Clarke. "Mabel Parker little dreams how near chance has come to cutting short the career of one who proposes to do her the honor of becoming her husband."

Chapter V.

A Conference.

When Zack and his companion came within sight of the house, the boy began to exhibit symptoms of uneasiness, and he slackened his pace.

"What's the matter?" inquired Clarke.

"I'm afraid they'll see me with this gun," said Zack. "I hadn't oughter have it, and Mehitable's got sharp eyes. If you'd just as lieves wait a minute, I'll just dodge along and put it away."

"Very well," said Clarke. "But who's Mehitable?"

"She's an old maid that does the kitchen work. She's as homely as a board fence, but she thinks she's handsome and that somebody will come along and marry her, some day."

"Humph!" said Clarke. "On the whole, my boy, you needn't trouble yourself to come back. I can just as well go up and announce myself."

Feeling relieved by this assurance, Zack proceeded to make his way stealthily to the building from which he had taken the gun. But fate was against him. Mehitable had gone out a moment before to get some chips with which to replenish the fire and met Zack, face to face, as he was entering.

"O, you wicked, wicked boy," she commenced in a shrill voice. "Who gave you leave, I'd like to know, to carry off this gun?"

"Hush, Hitty," said Zack in a mysterious voice. "I met a stranger in the woods who came up to the house with me. I reckon he's in search of a wife, and if you run right in, you'll get a chance to open the front door and let him in. And who knows what may happen if he likes your looks?"

"What sort of a looking man is he?" asked Mehitable, her curiosity and interest aroused. "How old is he?"

"About your age I guess. It would make a capital match."

"I ain't certain as it would be right for me to marry after disappinting poor Joshua," said Mehitable pensively. "Is he—does he look as if he was pretty well off?"

"There he is knocking at the door. Run, or you won't see him."

Forgetful of her dignity, Mehitable paid heed to this recommendation, and a moment afterwards presented herself at the door to admit the stranger.

"This is Mehitable," thought Clarke. "It's just as well to get into her good graces. I may hereafter have need of her assistance."

"Mrs. Parker, I presume?" he said with a deferential bow.

"No, sir," said Mehitable, fluttering with pleasure at being mistaken for the mistress of the household. "Mr. Parker is a widderer."

"Ah, indeed! A lady friend, then I presume. May I inquire if Mr. Parker is in at this time?"

"What a polite gentleman he is!" thought Mehitable. "I was always told that I was very lady-like, and he seems to be a good judge.—Won't you walk in, sir, while I go and see?" she said aloud in the most gracious manner.

"I think I will remain at the door. I am sorry to give you so much trouble."

"O, no trouble at all, sir," and Mehitable tripped away with as much grace and lightness as could be expected of a maiden of forty-seven.

Joseph Parker was sitting in the east room, so called, an apartment which was devoted principally to his use. The room was furnished more after the fashion of a city residence than a log cabin. A carpet covered the floor. The chairs were of mahogany, curiously carved. One or two family portraits hung on the wall, and, arranged on shelves, was a collection of some forty or fifty volumes. Mr. Parker himself was sitting at the window, out of which he gazed with a look which plainly took in little of the beauty that was spread out before him. There was a listless look upon his face which betokened a spirit not at rest. Something he craved which the wilderness could not give him. Labor being repugnant to him, he managed his clearing through others, while his own energies were left without any field in which to exercise themselves.

"There's a gentleman at the door that wants to see you," said Mehitable, abruptly opening the door.

"A gentleman to see me!" repeated Mr. Parker with some surprise. "Very well, you may show him in."

Clarke entered the room with an affable smile and bowed deferentially.

"Good morning, sir," said Mr. Parker hesitatingly.

"I see you don't remember me, sir. It is not strange, as I believe, though your person has long been familiar to me, that I have never had the pleasure of exchanging a word with you. By way of introduction, let me announce myself as Richard Clarke of New York, an humble disciple of that profession which counts so many master minds among its devoted—I mean the law."

"You are a lawyer, then, Mr. Clarke?" said Mr. Parker. "Have you come here with an intention of establishing yourself?"

"No, sir, I confess to a preference for the more thickly settled part of the country. You will perhaps be surprised when I tell you that my sole motive in making this somewhat arduous journey is connected with yourself."

"With me!" exclaimed Squire Parker, lifting his eyes in profound astonishment.

"It is even as I say," said the lawyer. "I may add that my visit may redound to your advantage. This, however, depends in a great measure on the manner in which you receive what I have to say."

"Proceed, sir," said Mr. Parker. "You have aroused my interest."

"Before doing so," said Clarke, "I will recapitulate some events in your past history, that you may perceive how far I comprehend your present position. We shall then be better prepared to understand each other."

The lawyer, for henceforth this will be the readiest name by which to distinguish our acquaintance, at once commenced his narrative.

"I am perfectly well aware that, though at present an occupant of a cabin in the wilderness, you were born to wealth and social distinction, which but for untoward circumstances would still be in your possession. Your father held a high colonial office previous to the struggle which eventuated in sundering the present states from the mother country. Although in that struggle he aimed to preserve neutrality, I believe I am correct in saying that his sympathies were rather with England than the colonies."

"I believe such to have been the case," said Mr. Parker.

"This point is immaterial. One of the acts to which it led, however, is of the highest importance. But before speaking of this, let me go on with my brief narrative. I believe your father's death was sudden."

"It was. He was suddenly struck with apoplexy which, though not immediately fatal, deprived him of speech, so that during the short time he had to live he was unable to communicate with me."

"He appeared to have something on his mind which he wished to communicate?" said the lawyer with a certain degree of eagerness in his manner.

"He did, and seemed to be quite distressed to think that it was out of his power to do so. But sir—improbable as it appears, your manner leads me to ask the question—have you any conjecture as to the nature of this communication which my father was prevented from making?"

"As to that, Squire Parker, I may have or I may not. You will excuse me for being non-committal just at present.

Remember that I am a lawyer and that is a part of our trade. I have a question or two more to ask."

"Your manner is somewhat mysterious," said Mr. Parker with some hauteur. "However, I will take it for granted that you have a sufficient motive for it, and will answer any questions of a proper nature which you have to ask."

"It is only what I expected from a man of your intelligence," said the lawyer affably. "I will endeavor not to trouble you with any unnecessary questions."

"Go on, Mr. Clarke," said Mr. Parker, exhibiting a degree of impatience in his tone.

"Did your father leave as much property as you anticipated?"

Mr. Parker looked at the lawyer in some surprise, the question not being of such a character as he was led to expect.

"There is no reason," he said, after a pause, "why I should not answer this question of yours, although I cannot guess your object in asking it. I frankly admit, then, that I was surprised to find the property less by one half than I had supposed. However, nothing is more common than that the public opinion should exaggerate the amount of property belonging to a person known to be wealthy. As I had never heard my father allude directly to the extent of his possessions, I was led to the conclusion that, in common with the public, I had been mistaken on the subject or else, which was by no means improbable, that in the troubles of that stormy period my father's wealth had been diminished by losses."

"The conjecture was a plausible one," said the lawyer, "but that which is plausible is not necessarily correct. Did it never occur to you that it might be upon this subject that your father wished to speak to you when suffering under the attack which proved fatal to him?"

"I have formed many conjectures on the subject," said Mr. Parker, scanning the lawyer's face with interest, "but I confess that this never occurred to me. Have you any reason to suppose—your look seems to indicate it—that such is the case?"

"I have," said the lawyer briefly.

"And of what nature is this evidence?" asked Mr. Parker. "Is it so decisive as to promise any advantageous results?"

"I have no hesitation is saying that it is."

"I wait your further disclosures with impatience, Mr. Clarke."

"I must ask you to restrain your impatience for a moment. I think I have heard that of the diminished property which came into your possession, you were unfortunate enough to lose a large part. Is this the case?"

"The circumstances under which you see me living," said Mr. Parker with some bitterness, "will be a sufficient reply to your question."

"I did not know but your retirement to this romantic spot, which though a wilderness has much of natural beauty, was dictated by a preference for country life."

"No, sir, far from it. I am not a sentimentalist. I have no taste for the country or country life. I was born in a city, or at all events a considerable town which is now a city, and should never have left it if I could have continued to live there in the style to which I had been accustomed from my birth. But that could not be. The money which I inherited from my father, amounting to fifty thousand dollars, I was unwise enough to invest in speculations which promised large returns, although I ought to have been contented with the safer but apparently less productive investments which my father had employed. Well, sir, I need not enter into details. Enough that I found myself reduced, two years since, to a comparative pittance through the failure of the schemes in which I had trusted. I could no longer live in New York, save in the most humble way, and that the family pride which came to me with my inheritance would not brook. I had no mind to see myself looked down upon by those whom I had associated with as my equals, perhaps as my inferiors, and, hard as the sacrifice was, I determined to cut loose the ties which bound me to my native place and seek an humble asylum in this frontier district. I did not expect to find happiness here, nor have I been disappointed. I find myself cut off from all the associations to which I had been accustomed and forced to take up a life which has but a single redeeming trait. This is that I have removed myself far beyond the pity, indifference, or neglect of those whom I before knew. I have also the satisfaction of seeing that my daughter takes the change more kindly than myself. I am not sure even but she prefers her present life to that of the city. I cannot comprehend it. I think she must differ essentially in tastes and temperament from myself."

This the father said musingly.

"I think I could explain it," thought the lawyer. "I am very much afraid she is in love with this young Davenport. Lovers, at her age, are very apt to overlook all else."

"Well, sir," resumed Mr. Parker, "I have now expressed myself at greater length than I intended in relation to my position here, and how I look upon it. I am now ready and anxious to hear anything which you may be able to communicate upon the subject."

"I will come to the point at once, sir," said the lawyer, "by stating that I have the power of replacing you in your old position and enabling you to reappear among your former friends and associates with the same advantages of wealth, the loss of which has driven you to seek a home in the wilderness."

Mr. Parker was not prepared for this revelation. It seemed too strange, too improbable to be true. And yet if it should! His face flushed with new-born hope, his lips parted in eagerness, and in an agitated tone he said, "Surely you will not mock me with delusive hopes?"

"Surely not, Mr. Parker," said the lawyer scanning him narrowly. "I promise nothing which I am not abundantly able to perform."

"But this seems so mysterious! How can you, a stranger, possess this power of which you speak?"

"Chance, sir, has thrown it into my way. But as you will naturally enough desire a confirmation of my words, I will so

31

far task your patience as to relate briefly the manner in which certain facts, having a weighty bearing upon your interests, became known to me."

"Do so, sir. I am all attention."

Chapter VI.

The Hidden Treasure.

"When you left the city a year or two since," commenced the lawyer, "you sold out a large part of your furniture at auction."

"All except the little that you see in this room, with a few other articles."

"So I understand. Among those who were attracted to the auction by curiosity or the desire of making purchases was myself. I did not enjoy the acquaintance of yourself or your accomplished daughter, though I was familiar with both by sight. I was not tempted to purchase until a desk of antique pattern was put up by the auctioneer. Finding it going at a low figure and having need of an article of the kind, I ventured to bid upon it and it was knocked down to me."

"Then you were the purchaser?" said Mr. Parker, looking up suddenly.

"I was," returned the lawyer, a little surprised.

"It was one of the few articles," explained Mr. Parker, "which I intended to reserve, but owing to some misunderstanding between the auctioneer and myself, my direction was not followed. If either my daughter or myself had been present, we should have forbidden the sale, but for reasons which you will readily guess the thought of being present was a painful one and we were both out of the city. When I returned the next day, I desired to obtain it back, even at a large advance, but found that the auctioneer retained no recollection either of the name or person of the purchaser, and entry had been made only of the amount for which it sold. If you would be willing to sell it at any reasonable valuation, I should be glad to purchase it back."

"I will set no valuation upon it, Mr. Parker, but, without consideration of any kind, will, with pleasure, forward it to you when I return to New York, if indeed I am not favored with your company thither."

"I acknowledge your courtesy," said Mr. Parker with a degree of reserve, "but I should prefer at least to pay you the sum which you gave for it."

"That was so trifling that the use of the desk has already reimbursed me."

"Then, sir," said Mr. Parker with a degree of reluctance still perceptible in his tone, "it only remains for me to accept your obliging proposal. But you will pardon my interruption and proceed with your narrative."

"For a considerable time," resumed the lawyer, "I made use of the desk without feeling any especial curiosity about it. It lay on the table in my office and proved extremely serviceable. But one day curiosity led me to examine with more particularity the numerous little drawers and compartments which it contained, and while thus engaged my finger chanced to press a secret spring which at once revealed the presence of a drawer whose existence I had not before suspected."

"Indeed this is new to me," said Mr. Parker with visible surprise.

"Then your father never communicated to you that the desk contained such a drawer?"

"Never."

"I need scarcely have asked the question, however, as otherwise you would have made the discovery which it was reserved to me to stumble upon."

"A discovery!"

"Yes, and one of moment, as you will admit."

"Its nature?" questioned Mr. Parker, fixing his eyes eagerly upon the lawyer.

"The drawer, which was a small one, contained a closely written paper in which your father went on to say that, in the troubled state of the period,—you know at his death the revolutionary struggle was not decided—I say, in consideration of the unsettled state of politics, he had decided as a measure of proper precaution to conceal in a secure hiding place one half of his property which he had with that design converted into gold."

"Indeed," said Mr. Parker with an air of surprise. "I had not suspected it. It was in relation to this, no doubt, that my father desired to speak to me when he was so suddenly seized."

"You are, no doubt, correct."

"However, it has not been allowed to remain a secret. I suppose the place of concealment was mentioned."

"It was," answered the lawyer briefly.

Mr. Parker looked expectant, awaiting the revelation. But the lawyer was not inclined to speak.

A little surprised, he said, after a pause, "And this place?"

"My dear sir," said the lawyer, "I may as well be frank with you. I consider this document as a sort of treasure trove to which the finder is not without claim."

"Would you lay claim to my inheritance?" exclaimed Mr. Parker with indignation.

"Pardon my bungling mode of expression," said Clarke. "You have misunderstood me, but it is my fault. I mean that it is only to be expected that I should wish to reap a little advantage from this windfall of Fortune."

"In other words, you think you ought to receive some reward for your agency in this matter?"

"You have expressed my meaning, Mr. Parker. You know, sir, we professional men are apt to regard such things in a professional point of view, and however it may be with others, I do not pretend to be above the weaknesses of humanity."

"Of that, sir, I have no disposition to complain. I trust I am too much of a gentleman to be guilty of the meanness of leaving you without compensation for so essential a service as this."

"Thank you, sir. I felt sure that such would be your sentiments."

"The only thing that remains, then, is to fix upon the amount of compensation. Would you regard two thousand dollars as sufficient?"

The lawyer cast down his eyes and was silent.

"I see that you do not so consider it," pursued Mr. Parker. "Although I do not absolutely promise to accede to your proposal, yet I should wish you to be satisfied. Will you therefore have the goodness yourself to name the compensation which you would consider sufficient?"

Again the lawyer hesitated, as if in doubt.

"The compensation which I desire," he said at length, "is perhaps of a different nature from that which you anticipate."

He paused again and Mr. Parker, though surprised, signed for him to go on.

"You have a daughter, Squire Parker?"

"Assuredly, though what she can have to do with this business is more than I can understand."

"I remember your daughter as she appeared in the city. I used to meet her every day on her way to and from school. She is very beautiful."

"I think Mr. ——, ahem, Mr. Clarke—that it is a business matter that we are discussing," said Mr. Parker dryly.

"Very true, sir. I have, by no means, lost sight of that. As you are evidently impatient for me to come to a conclusion, I will state, as explicitly as it is in my power, that the only reward I seek is the hand of your daughter in marriage."

"Sir!" exclaimed Mr. Parker, rising in indignant surprise and looking down upon the attorney with infinite astonishment blended with scorn. "Do I hear aright? Is it the hand of my daughter that—that—"

"That I seek in marriage," suggested the lawyer coolly. "You are quite correct."

36

"Who are you, sir? What is your pedigree that you should have the presumption to make such a proposal?"

"As for my pedigree, I take it that it corresponds with yours when you get far enough up. We are both, I believe, descended from Adam, or if you want to come nearer, I think it probable that Noah is our common ancestor."

"Do you mean to insult me, sir?" said Mr. Parker hotly.

"It certainly would not be very decorous to insult a man whom I have invited to become my father-in-law."

"Probably this is a jest. I regret that it should prove such a sorry one. I am willing to forget it and will now ask you again to fix upon some compensation which you will consider adequate."

"Squire Parker," returned his visitor firmly, "I am not in the habit of jesting, and I am in the habit of saying what I mean. I repeat, then, that I am willing to put you in possession of this sum of fifty thousand dollars—a sum which will enable you to return to the city and resume your former style of living—on this condition alone, that you give me the hand of your daughter in marriage."

Mr. Parker paced the room in no little agitation. He was of what is conventionally designated as a high family, and his pride and prejudices both revolted against the proposed union of his daughter with an obscure lawyer of no lineage. It is to be feared that this consideration weighed with him far more seriously than the thought of incompatibility in respect to age and other important respects by which his daughter's happiness would be likely to be imperilled. Like many at that day, he considered love to be but a secondary matter in a marriage contract, and considerations of family and fortune of paramount importance. I have thought it necessary to enter into this explanation in order that the full force of Mr. Parker's objections may be apprehended.

The lawyer watched him narrowly as he paced the room and easily penetrated the nature of this struggle through which he was passing. At the same time he thought he perceived that Mr. Parker was a selfish as well as a proud man, and it was on this that he counted for the ultimate consent which he fully expected to gain.

"I know what the old fellow is thinking of me" passed through his mind. "He, no doubt, regards me as a mere nobody—as a vulgar adventurer perhaps—and considers it probably as a piece of the most flagrant presumption, on my part, to aspire to the hand of his daughter. The pride of these old aristocrats is perfectly measureless. Strip them of everything else, and that remains. Well, I can wait till he has made up his mind in my favor. I have no fear but he will do it, sooner or later."

By this time Mr. Parker had made up his mind to another appeal.

"I think," he said, addressing the lawyer, "that I understand your motive in proposing my daughter's hand as the condition of revealing the information of which you have come into clandestine possession."

"Allow me to correct your phraseology, sir," said the lawyer mildly. "The word clandestine conveys a suspicion of my honor, to which as a matter of course I object. Suppose you substitute the word accidental as more befitting the actual circumstances."

"Very well, sir," said Mr. Parker, biting his lips. "I repeat, then, that I think I comprehend the motive which prompts you to make application for my daughter's hand. You think then to extort from me—"

"Extort!"

"Obtain, then, from me a larger sum for the information of which you have come into accidental possession."

"My dear sir, you greatly underrate your daughter's attractions, if you think that I have introduced her in this way."

Not heeding this disclaimer, Mr. Parker proceeded: "This being the case I yet feel that I am, to a certain extent, in your power. You have, honorable or otherwise, I will not say, obtained a hold upon me. If you choose to demand an exorbitant price for your information, I am compelled to submit to your terms."

"You do accept my terms!" exclaimed the lawyer eagerly.

"You are too fast, sir," said Mr. Parker coldly. "I so far yield to your demands that I will agree to give you the marriage portion which I should design to bestow with my daughter, this being, as I conceive, what you really are aiming at. That portion will be ten thousand dollars, or one fifth of the property of which I expect to come into possession."

"I regard the marriage portion as liberal, Mr. Parker," was the lawyer's reply, "but in one point I grieve to disappoint you. I should, of course, expect to receive a marriage portion with your daughter, but I must insist on her going with it."

Mr. Parker drew back haughtily. "Sir," he said, "I regret to find you so persistent in refusing what I regard as an unusually favorable offer on my part. You must be aware that in respect of birth and station my daughter is no suitable match for you."

"I frankly admit it" was the unexpected reply, "and perhaps it is for this reason that I feel a strong desire to mate myself with one who possesses what I lack. I desire to elevate myself by marriage, and circumstances have pointed to your daughter as the one to whom I can, with the most propriety, look for a member of such a partnership. Her uncommon personal attractions of course recommend her further, and therefore I shall continue to insist on this point."

"And if I break off the negotiation peremptorily and forever?" demanded Mr. Parker. "You will then have gained nothing by your discovery."

"Pardon me," said the lawyer coolly. "You appear to forget one very important circumstance."

"And what is that?"

"I know where the money is concealed."

"Good Heavens! You would not possess yourself of it to the exclusion of the true owner."

"I certainly would. Indeed I take credit to myself for not having done so without speaking to you on the subject at all. You must allow that you at least would never have been the wiser nor have had the slightest suspicion that you had met with a loss."

Mr. Parker groaned and covered his face with his hands as he realized the truth of these words and the extent to which therefore he was in the power of the man before him.

"However," pursued Clarke coolly, "I did not do as I have said I might, for more than one reason, perhaps, but it certainly was not the least that I hoped to become your son-in-law, and I have the good taste to value youth and beauty above the mere dross of gold, which however is a very good thing in its way. But, sir, I see that, in an event of this importance, you are naturally unable to decide at a moment's notice. I will therefore retire for the present and take another opportunity of calling upon you. In the meantime I shall take up my residence at the tavern in the village, where you can readily hear of me if you should desire to confer further on this important subject. I have the pleasure of wishing you a good morning."

Mr. Parker did not appear to notice the departure of his guest but remained for a long time in the same position, his mind a prey to conflicting thoughts and emotions.

Chapter VII.

A Lover's Confession.

About a quarter of a mile from the cabin, the lawyer's attention was drawn to a youthful couple who were chatting gaily, each seemingly fully occupied with the other. They were engaged in a playful altercation, the young man having begged the gift of a wild rose which his companion held laughingly out of his reach.

"But why won't you give it to me, Mabel?" pleaded the young man.

"Why won't I, sir? Because you are altogether too acquisitive. Why should you deprive me of my poor little rose when there are so many others on the bushes close by?"

"But they are not the same to me, Mabel."

The lively girl pretended to misunderstand him while his persistence really pleased her.

"You mean that I have helped myself to the best one. For shame, Henry, to accuse me of such selfishness."

"Well, Mabel, I will make you a proposal."

"Hadn't you better make it to Mehitable?" said Mabel slyly.

"Pshaw. I was going to say that I would get another rose and then exchange with you."

"I don't see what advantage there would be in that," said Mabel with provoking obtuseness.

"But you will agree to it, nevertheless."

"No, sir, I shall not encourage you in your whims. It is time you began to exercise a little self-denial."

"But you know I am not used to that."

"So much the better. Perhaps under my training I may be able to make something of you."

"Will you indeed take me under your training?" asked the young man earnestly.

"I fear it would be too great an undertaking," said she, shaking her head. "I am afraid you would make a very troublesome responsibility. Perhaps Mehitable—"

"Confound Mehitable!"

"What has poor Mehitable done? Do you think I will stand still and hear her abused?"

"I have no doubt she is a very estimable old lady, but—"

"Old lady! It would be hardly safe for her to hear you speak of her thus. By her own account she is only about thirty."

"Heaven preserve her, then, from ever living till sixty. She will look old enough to be the great-grandmother of all living."

"Poor Mehitable! I see you have a prejudice against her. But how we have been wasting our time! If you will come to the cabin with me, I will give you some cake of my own making."

"That will certainly be a powerful inducement. But why need we be in haste. It is so much pleasanter here in the open air."

"I don't feel as if my friendship for Mehitable should permit me to remain longer with one who is so wanting in appreciation of her charms."

"But, Mabel," said the young man, "I am ready to make amends for that."

"How? By proposing to the young lady? I think she will accept you."

"How provoking you are, Mabel! But since you have tempted me, I am going to be guilty of an act of daring."

"I! Tempted you to an act of daring. I think, Henry, that you overrate my influence!"

"You are quite incorrigible!"

42

"I am glad you admit it. Now you will see how hopeless a task it will be to attempt reforming me."

While the latter part of the conversation was going on, they had gradually advanced to the base of an old tree of huge proportions—a perfect Titan among forest trees—under which for convenience's sake had been erected a seat.

"Sit down a moment, Mabel," said young Davenport with a sudden change of tone. "There is something I have wished to say to you a long time. I feel that the time has come for saying it now."

"Perhaps you are about to confess some guilt that lies heavy on your soul," said Mabel lightly, though her heart beat faster than its wont, for with the subtle premonition of a true woman she felt what it was that Henry Davenport was about to say.

"I am indeed about to make a confession," said the youth seriously, seating himself beside her.

She did not venture to look up, for she knew that she could not meet the steady gaze of his eyes without betraying her own feelings.

"I am ready to be your confessor," she returned, while mechanically she began to pull apart the rose which had been the subject of dispute between them.

"I hope, Mabel, that you are not unprepared to hear that I love you," said the young man abruptly. "Pardon my coming to the point so bluntly, but I cannot help following the bent of my feelings."

The roses were brighter than ever on Mabel's cheeks, but she could not avoid giving way to her natural archness.

"It is a worse offence than I anticipated," she said, "but if you do truly and sincerely repent of it, I may extend you my forgiveness."

"No, no," said the young man eagerly. "I do not feel the slightest particle of repentance."

"But, perhaps, if you make a slight effort—"

"Pardon me, that I have no intention of doing."

"Then," said Mabel demurely, "I am afraid I shall have to forgive you on your own terms."

She looked so attractive at that moment, her eyes half veiled in maiden shyness, her cheeks tinged with a crimson flush, and her answer conveyed so much hope and encouragement that our hero may be pardoned for yielding to the sudden temptation to which he was subjected and stealing a kiss.

The action was so sudden that he was completely successful.

"How dare you, Henry?" exclaimed Mabel, who was not however very seriously offended, when her rebuke was cut short in an unexpected manner.

The sound of a laugh, half suppressed and suddenly checked, smote upon the ears of both at the same moment. Mabel, with a deep blush, separated herself from the embrace of her lover and looked about her with an air of confusion. The young man started to his feet and looked in various directions for the author of the unpleasant interruption. But no one appeared to be in sight.

"Didn't you hear a noise, Mabel?"

"Yes."

"That sounded like one laughing."

"Yes."

At this moment a rustling caught the attention of both and revealed the whereabouts of the spy upon their privacy.

Perched among the branches of a tree at a little distance was the boy Zack.

Now it is not very pleasant to be disturbed in an agreeable tête à tête and it was in a stern tone that Henry Davenport called out, "What mischief are you doing up there?"

"I ain't doing any mischief," said Zack boldly.

"Then why did you go up there? What other inducement could you have?"

"There's a good prospect from here, Mr. Davenport," said Zack, laughing out of the corner of his eye.

"Humph!" said the young man, coloring. "That is no answer to my question."

"I ain't responsible to you, as I know of," said Zack. "I'll answer Miss Mabel there, though perhaps it's all the same."

This was said in so droll and knowing a tone that neither Henry nor Mabel could help laughing.

"Well, Zack, come down and I will give you something," said the young man good humoredly.

"A licking perhaps?" suggested the wily Zack, not stirring.

"No, Zack, of course you wouldn't stand in need of that. But here's half a dollar for you."

At sight of the coin Zack slid down the tree with wonderful rapidity and presented himself before the young man.

"Of course, Zack," said Henry, "you know that we feel an interest in you, and *if you behave well* you may get another."

Zack perfectly well understood what was implied in the expression emphasized, and signified as much by a very knowing wink.

"I understand, Mr. Davenport," said he. "It ain't always necessary to tell what a feller sees. Did I tell you that Mehitable thinks she's got a beau?"

"Mehitable got a beau!" exclaimed Mabel, forgetting her own embarassment.

"Just ask her, if you don't believe me," said Zack.

Chapter VIII.

Second Thoughts.

The lawyer's visit had operated upon Mr. Parker as a stone thrown into a pool, producing movement and agitation, a general feeling of unrest which time alone could calm. There are some natures that seem made for a particular sphere and are not pliant enough to adapt themselves to the requisitions of another. So it was with him. He had been bred to all the privileges which wealth and high birth bestow, and in a quiet way had been in the habit of looking down upon all who did not move in the same circle with himself. He was one of those who cherish a devout belief in the superiority of gentle blood, and still felt a secret longing for the old continental regime when such things possessed a higher value than afterwards.

To such a man the sudden downfall which has already been described proved a severe blow. The thought of ranking with those whom he had regarded with condescension only, and of being treated as an inferior by those with whom he had hitherto moved on terms of perfect equality, was indeed bitter to one of his disposition. He could no longer endure to live where he would be subjected to such mortifications. But for this imperative reason he never would have brought himself to what in his case might be fairly considered a desperate step—namely, a home in the western wilderness. It was a sacrifice which he made upon the altar of his pride, but when the change was once effected, although it had the advantage of removing him from daily recurring scenes and encounters in which his proud spirit would have chafed, it was very far from bringing positive happiness or content. He had indeed exhibited a little interest in fitting up the cabin, but after that was completed he sank into a state of restlessness and lethargy which gave Mabel, when she observed it, a vague feeling of uneasiness. But she herself was so thoroughly contented with the change that she was unable to enter into her father's feelings. She had no longings after the old life which she had led in the city. Compared with the wild, free life of the woods it had lost all its attractions. This was particularly the case after her acquaintance with Henry Davenport had ripened into an intimacy which led to their being almost daily together. At first, probably neither knew how strong was the liking for the other's society. Love is born in unconsciousness. The discovery that another has become necessary to one's happiness is not made till long after the fact has become established.

Both Henry and Mabel had many tastes in common. They delighted in long walks or gallops upon the soft turf and scarcely a day passed without some such mutual engagement. In addition to this, young Davenport had placed a boat on the little sheet of water near the cabin and would often row his fair companion across it. He had even taught her to manage an oar with considerable dexterity, so that she would sometimes laughingly order him to take his turn as passenger while she plied the oars. Entering into the humor of the jest, he would lie luxuriously back and watch the short, quick strokes of his fair companion, not without admiring the plump and rounded arms or the animated countenance flushing with exercise and beaming with enjoyment.

But Mr. Parker had no such pleasant associations with the country. The cultivation of land with all the wonderful phenomena of vegetation he regarded as irksome but essential to the support of the family. He therefore committed it to other hands, nor did he even reserve to himself the general superintendence of the farming operations, for which indeed he was as little fitted by experience as by inclination. No wonder, therefore, that he spent his time in restless discontent and vain longings after the life which he had left behind him in the city.

As long as he regarded his present state as inevitable, these feelings were kept under some restraint and he submitted, though with an ill grace to what he knew no complaints could remedy. But after his conversation with the lawyer, the feeling of disgust for his present circumstances and yearning for the past came over him with redoubled force. The longer he thought of the possibility which existed of regaining what he so much coveted, the more desirable it seemed—the more unendurable it appeared to get along without [it].

"To think," he murmured to himself as he paced his apartment with hasty steps and a flush upon his usually pale cheek, "to think that I may again live in the old mansion—which I was compelled to surrender—that I may again keep my carriage and entertain my old friends and live as befits a gentleman of my rank and breeding! Ah, that will be living indeed! I would gladly shake off all thoughts of this hut in which I have been compelled to immure myself. Living here is only vegetating. One year of my former life is worth five, nay ten in this out-of-the-way place where I am deprived of all that I value. Yes, I may get it all back. He says so, and though he is not a gentleman, his story is a plausible one. But the condition—"

Here his countenance changed, and with some heat he exclaimed: "The low-born fellow has actually the audacity to demand Mabel's hand in marriage and to make that the condition of restoring me to what is rightfully my own. I have a great mind to have him arrested."

A moment's reflection was sufficient to convince Mr. Parker that such a proceeding would be ill-advised inasmuch as he would be utterly unable to prove anything. The lawyer would undoubtedly meet his charges with a cool denial. He could hardly be expected to admit anything to his own detriment.

What then could be done!

There seemed to be but a single alternative, since the conversation recorded in the last chapter had left no room for doubt as to the strength of the lawyer's determination.

This alternative was—either to give up all thought of obtaining the money and its contingent advantages, or to submit to the condition imposed.

The last Mr. Parker could not at first endure to think of. But being a man who had been accustomed, through life, to regard his own comfort and advantage of paramount importance, he began, little by little, to reconcile himself to it. This he was the better able to do because the objection arose merely from his own prejudice, not his regard to his daughter's feelings. The matter then ultimately resolved itself to this, and in this form he submitted it to himself for consideration.

Would it be a greater sacrifice for him to put up with an unacceptable son-in-law, or to spend the remainder of his life in a wilderness and a state of society which he detested?

It was not difficult to decide what the answer would be. It required only a little time to arrive at it.

The lawyer had had the foresight to see this, and for this reason he had had the good policy not to insist upon an immediate answer to his proposition, but to give time for Mr. Parker's selfishness to present the matter in its bearing upon his own comfort.

After Mr. Parker had begun to reconcile himself to that branch of the alternative which would require from him the least sacrifice, the process became rapid.

"After all," he thought, "there is nothing in this man's profession which should interfere with his being a gentleman, and if he is lacking in pedigree, the deficiency can easily be supplied by money. It can be reported that he has high connections in England, and as no one will take the trouble to go over to ascertain the incorrectness of the report, it will pass unquestioned. It is, I admit, presumption in him to make the demand. Still, it is better to sacrifice a little pride for the sake of a great advantage. And besides I don't know that Mabel is likely to make a more advantageous connection in this wild place."

It is to be observed that Mr. Parker had never suspected the strong interest felt by young Davenport, nor indeed, so much had his time been devoted to brooding over his own peculiar troubles, had he probably noticed the extent to which their intimacy had gone. He did not, therefore, anticipate the disarrangement which his plans were likely to receive from this source.

But this discovery was not long to be delayed. The avowal of love which had been made by Henry Davenport was followed by a subsequent conversation in which both parties agreed to make the matter known to their respective families. The necessity of this communication troubled neither. No opposition was anticipated as both the families were on intimate terms, and in other respects there seemed to be no great difference except that Mr. Davenport was unquestionably much the wealthier. But as he had no aristocratic prejudices to contend against, it was not likely that this would have any effect upon his mind. Besides, Mr. Parker,—though he could not have commanded more than a thousand dollars for his whole estate, real and personal,—was in comfortable, nay superior circumstances for that part of the country. Undoubtedly, Mr. Davenport would be glad to find that his son had formed an attachment to one fitted by education and culture, as well as personal attractions, to dignify his choice.

"Father," said Mabel in a tone of hesitation arising from the knowledge of the purpose for which she soliticed an interview, "I should be glad to see you in the study a few minutes."

"Certainly," said her father, surprised that she should have anticipated a request which he had himself thought of making.

Mehitable heard this request through the half open door,

and the curiosity of the handmaiden—a quality of which she had her share—was greatly excited.

"I wonder what she's got to say to her father," thought that lady. "Maybe she's going to complain of me. She told me yesterday that she thought the meat was overdone. A pretty chit she is to talk to me who knew all about cooking before she was born."

Mehitable forgot that her expressions were of a nature to throw doubt upon her often asserted claims to juvenility. However, it is perhaps too much to expect one at all times to be consistent—and we will not exact too much of Mehitable in this respect.

In compliance with his daughter's request, Mr. Parker proceeded to the study, as the room was generally called which was appropriated as before described to his use.

Mabel followed with a flushed cheek yet with a happy light in her eye. She dreaded the task of opening to her father the subject of her love, yet she would not for a large sum have forgone the occasion of her embarrassment.

"I'd like to know that it is they're going to talk about," repeated Mehitable, as she prepared to clear away the table. "P'r'aps Mr. Parker may say something about that fine young man that came here yesterday and seemed so struck with my appearance. I'd give a good deal to know who he is, and what is his business with the Squire, and whether he thinks of settling down in this deestrict of country, and whether he's married, though I don't think he is, and whether he isn't in search of a wife."

Mehitable's volubility in wondering was very great, but it was at least fully equalled by her curiosity. Accustomed as she had been for many years past to consider, in regard to every man, whether he was available in a matrimonial way, the politeness of the lawyer, stimulated by Zack's hint, had worked upon her imagination to such an extent that she was already half persuaded that it required but an effort upon her part to bring the lawyer to her feet. That effort she was willing to make.

"Poor man! perhaps he's had a misfortunate attachment like my Joshua that I rejected because I didn't love him. But I'm sure I didn't object to somebody's else making him happy, pervided he could make up his mind to like another arter his disappintment—. So I think if I could see it to be my duty, that I should be willing to marry the gentleman that seems so pretty and polite in his manner. I can't say but what I'd like to have a house of my own. There's some satisfaction in working for yourself and your own family that there isn't in working for other people that don't know how to appreciate you."

There thoughts passed through Mehitable's mind in much less time than I have consumed in recording them and were terminated by the closing of the door after Mabel and her father.

"I wonder if I couldn't creep up to the door and hear what they're a sayin'," thought Mehitable to herself. "I've a great mind to. Mabel may say something about me and I like to know what people says about me. I guess I'll take the dust brush with me so's if their door should suddenly open, they'd think that I was a dustin'."

This plan recommended itself to Mehitable as the best she could adopt and she lost no time in putting it into execution.

"The dishes may stand," she muttered. "Zack hasn't had his breakfast, and though he don't deserve it, I guess I'll let the table wait for him a few minutes."

Seizing the dust brush, Mehitable passed cautiously into the entry, treading on tip toe and avoiding carefully even the least noise, intent upon gratifying her natural desire for information without the awkward accident of discovery.

She leaned her head forward, so that her eye was close to the key-hole, and in this attitude listened eagerly to what was said. What she heard was of even greater interest than she had anticipated.

But alas for Mehitable! in her plans of avoiding detection there was one element of uncertainty which she had quite forgotten to take note of.

This element of uncertainty assumed the form of a lively

boy already introduced to the reader under the name of Zack.

Now Zack had gone out early in the morning in search of birds' eggs, of which he had already collected quite a variety, and this made him late for breakfast.

Entering the kitchen with bare feet, he did not make sufficient noise to attract the attention of that lady. This was an unfortunate circumstance for her as it proved. Entering the kitchen Zack naturally looked about for Mehitable. Not finding her, he stepped to the entry door and there, to his surprise, found her in the act of eavesdropping.

This was quite a delightful discovery to Zack, who enjoyed nothing more than teasing the prim spinster, who on her side thought him the "boldest, most unbearable boy she ever set eyes upon."

"I'll fix her," thought Zack.

After pausing a minute or two, hoping that she would look up and learn to her confusion that she was discovered, Zack finally got tired of waiting and determined to precipitate matters.

Accordingly, he gave a slight cough which was sufficient, however, to draw Mehitable's attention.

Turning suddenly, she saw the boy looking at her with a whimsically knowing air which clearly indicated that he very well understood what she was about.

Mehitable started with a guilty look and her sallow face actually flushed.

"Why, Zack," said she in a flustered manner, "have you got back? I thought I'd let the breakfast things stand till you got back home, and as the entry needed dustin', I'd go to work dustin' it."

"Do you generally dust the key-hole, Hitty?" asked Zack, his eyes twinkling with mirth.

"What do you mean, Zachariah?" inquired Mehitable with offended dignity.

"O, I don't mean anything of course," said the provoking boy. "Only I saw you bending down with your ear close to the key-hole."

"I suppose you hain't any objection to my stoopin' over

and tyin' up my shoe string," said Mehitable in an injured tone.

"It took you pretty long to tie it, then. You didn't seem to be doing nothing for about five minutes while I was looking at you."

"O, you owdacious boy!" exclaimed the badgered spinster. "How do you dare to say such things about a poor unprotected girl that hasn't ever done you any harm. I've lived for years and years—"

"There isn't no doubt about that," said Zack with a meaning look.

"Don't you interrupt me, you little wretch. I ain't too old to be your sister."

"O, my gracious!" exclaimed Zack. "I should as soon think of being sister to my own grandmother."

"You can't have any coffee this morning," said Mehitable spitefully, "for it has got cold."

"Then you'll warm it for me," said Zack quietly.

"I will, will I? And who's to make me, I'd like to know."

"I am."

"You!" retorted Mehitable in a shrill voice, turning up her nose in effable contempt.

"Yes, that is, unless you'd like to have me tell Mabel about your listening at the door."

This produced another outburst from Mehitable, who nevertheless thought it most prudent to comply with the boy's demand—feeling that she had placed herself in his power. Nor was this the first occasion in which Mehitable had to rue the results of eavesdropping.

Chapter IX.

A Hard Alternative.

When the father and daughter found themselves together, a mutual feeling of embarrassment affected them, for both were considering in what way it would be best to open the conversation. At length the father spoke:

"I had a visitor yesterday, Mabel."

At that moment Mabel could only think of one person. She thought it possible that Henry Davenport, in his impatience to have the matter decided, might have called upon her father without her knowledge. In this case, her father's answer when she had requested a private interview could readily be understood.

"Was it Henry Davenport?" she asked in a low voice, endeavoring not to look unduly interested.

"Henry Davenport!" repeated Mr. Parker in some surprise. "Certainly not. I know of no especial reason for his calling. It was a lawyer from New York."

"Was he a middle-aged man of rather formidable aspect?" inquired Mabel.

"No," said Mr. Parker hesitating, for it was his desire that his daughter should look as favorably as possible on the stranger. "I should not describe him in that manner. He was not absolutely young, to be sure, nor I suppose what the ladies would call handsome, but you know beauty is not expected of a man."

"I won't quarrel with you on that point, father," said Mabel laughing, "nor oblige you to defend him. Whether he is as homely as a rail fence, or as handsome as an angel, he is nothing to me that I am aware of. I was only going to say that I caught a glimpse of him as he was walking in the direction of the tavern. I did not know that he had been here until I listened to Mehitable's enthusiastic praises of him after I returned. By her account he was very polite to her, and from the attention which she hints at, I judge that we must make up our minds to lose her. It would be a capital match, don't you think so?"

It was at this interesting point that Mehitable was compelled by the sudden discovery on the part of Zack, related in the previous chapter, to abandon her post. She would have given a good deal to hear what followed and never quite forgave Zack for disturbing her. The indifference with which Mabel spoke, however, relieved her from any fears of rivalry in the designs which she had already formed upon the lawyer's hand.

Mr. Parker, for obvious reasons, was not pleased with his daughter's manner of treating the subject. It promised ill for the sacrifice which he wished to propose to her.

"Mabel," said he with some severity of manner, "I shall be obliged to you to speak with less levity. To bring Mehitable into the conversation is entirely uncalled for, and the suggestion of a matrimonial connection between Mr. Clarke and a person occupying a menial position so far beneath his station in society is in the highest degree improper and might justly be regarded as an insult by him were he present to hear it."

"Father," said Mabel penitently, "you must pardon me for having spoken as you would not have me. I am naturally lively, and perhaps I have been carried too far. I certainly have, if I have incurred your displeasure."

"Mabel, my daughter," said the father affectionately, "you have ever been a good and dutiful daughter hitherto. I may, by and bye, make still another demand upon your duty. But I was speaking of my visitor of yesterday. Do you remember hearing of him when we lived in the city?"

"No, sir."

"He had seen you, however. But that is not to the purpose at present. Can you guess what was his errand?"

"No, sir. I suppose it could hardly be of a professional nature, as since your—." Mabel hesitated to say failure, knowing her father's sensitiveness upon this point.

"Since the great misfortune, you mean, which drove me out into this wilderness to lead a miserable existence, deprived of all the sources of my former happiness."

"Do you indeed take it so much to heart, father?" said Mabel, taking her father's hand and looking in his face with sympathy. "I wish you could feel as I do. It seems as if I never lived till now. I delight in the wild freedom of the woods and the unshackled life which I lead here. In the city one is so hemmed in by conventionalities that it is impossible to feel yourself quite independent. O my father, what can be more glorious than these stately forests and fertile fields? How beautiful it is to watch the sunrise from the hillock yonder. I could live here always without once longing for the old life that I led in the city."

"I don't pretend," said Mr. Parker peevishly, "to enter into your youthful enthusiasm, and I marvel much that a daughter of mine, the descendant of a lofty family with whom nobles have not infrequently intermarried, should be willing to confess such plebeian tastes. I cannot conceive what pleasure you can find in living in a miserable hut"— Mabel was about to utter an exclamation but prudently refrained—"a miserable hut built of logs, in the midst of a rude, uncultivated race of people who care nothing for good blood and fancy their plebeian stock as good as ours. I say I cannot conceal my astonishment that one so carefully reared should imbibe and give expression to such tastes. For my own part it has proved to me more unendurable than I anticipated. I remember once to have read an interesting account of a shipwrecked sailor named, I think, Robinson Crusoe, who was forced to live by himself on an uninhabited island. The book was written by one Defoe and was sent me in a package which was forwarded to me from London. I little thought when I read it that I was doomed, in my own person, to pass through a trial equally hard and to bear a solitude almost as intolerable."

"But, father, we have good neighbors, while Robinson Crusoe, if I remember rightly, was not so fortunate. You surely cannot compare your situation with his."

"Neighbors, Mabel? And what kind of neighbors? Do you think I can be on terms of intimacy with the rude, uncultivated settlers?"

"Surely you do not regard the Davenports in that light."

"No, they are exceptions, I admit. But it would take many such to supply to me the place of all that I enjoyed in the city."

Mabel felt that nothing she could say was likely to divert her father from the melancholy view which he now saw fit to express. She accordingly, after a minute's pause, endeavored to change the current of conversation by suggesting a question. "You were about to tell me on what business this lawyer came, were you not, father?"

"Yes, Mabel," said her father brightening up. "What will you say when I tell you that he has come to offer us the chance of resuming our old station in society,—that he has it in his power to restore us a measure of wealth equal to that which I inherited and lost."

"Father, you have excited my curiosity deeply. Can this indeed be as you say?"

"I do not wonder at your astonishment, Mabel. I was myself taken by surprise. But I can explain all in a very few words."

Mr. Parker here entered into an explanation of facts which are already familiar to the reader and which therefore do not require to be repeated. It is hardly necessary to say that Mabel listened with eager interest. The revelation gave her pleasure, but not for herself. The discontent which her father had expressed with the mode of life to which he was at present reduced led her, as a matter of course, to rejoice that means were provided for his restoration to the scenes which could alone content him. For her own part she had no desire to go back to the city and would have considered such a removal a great sacrifice. But her union with Henry Davenport would render this unnecessary, and although it would pain her to be entirely separated from her father, she had no doubt that an arrangement could be made by which she could pass a part of the year in the city. For the rest, her father would be contented in that sphere which he was prepared to value the more because of his temporary withdrawal from it.

It was therefore with a glow of pleasure that she said, "Father, I am indeed heartily glad for your sake that your losses are likely to be so amply made up to you, and I hereby acknowledge my penitence for having spoken somewhat disrespectfully of the lawyer who is the bearer of this welcome intelligence. I shall henceforth adopt the opinion that bad looks are no indication of a bad disposition. But, father, you will remember that I too have something to communicate."

"Yes, Mabel, I do remember that you solicited the interview. Pray speak without hesitation, and if it is any favor which it is in my power to grant, count it already granted."

"It is indeed a matter that vitally concerns my happiness, father," said Mabel in a low voice.

"Is it indeed so important?" said Mr. Parker, who as yet did not suspect the nature of the request which his daughter was about to make. "Indeed I cannot conjecture what it is. Tell me without reserve."

Mabel rose from her chair and sank at her father's feet in a childlike attitude.

"Father," she murmured, "I am very happy. Henry Davenport has told me that he loves me."

"Good Heavens!" exclaimed Mr. Parker in undisguised dismay. "Can this be true? And do you love him, Mabel?"

Startled by her father's manner, Mabel answered: "I love him as my life, father."

Rising hastily to his feet, Mr. Parker paced the room with knitted brow and disordered step. Mabel watched him with equal surprise and anxiety.

"Father," she at length said timidly, "I hope that you know nothing unfavorable of Henry."

"I do not," said Mr. Parker gloomily, pausing in his walk, "but, Mabel, this marriage, though it may bring happiness to you, can bring nothing but disaster and unhappiness to me."

"But, father, it need not separate us," said Mabel eagerly, supposing that her father's objection was founded upon this. "Henry could arrange to live in the city a part of the time."

"Child, you do not understand the matter. Your marriage with this young man would keep me a life-long prisoner in this odious wilderness."

"But why should it? Could you not support an establishment in the city, and now and then come out to visit your children? The property which are about to recover—"

"That property I shall never recover if you marry Henry Davenport," said her father gloomily.

"But what possible connection can there be between the two things?" questioned Mabel in perplexity. "Why should my marriage stand in the way of your recovering what is rightfully yours?"

"Sit down, Mabel—let us both sit—while I tell you. It is a circumstance which I regret nearly as much as you can. I have no personal objection to young Davenport. I would receive him gladly as a son-in-law, but there is one thing which I have yet to tell you. This lawyer demands a reward for his discovery of the letter which makes known to me the whereabouts of the treasure. That reward he has himself indicated. He has asked [for] you as his wife."

"But what can he know of me?" asked Mabel in amazement.

"More than you think. You remember that he belongs to New York—that he has lived there many years."

"But I never met him."

"Perhaps not as an acquaintance. But the daughter of Joseph Parker occupied a position which, as a matter of course, made her known to many with whom she was personally unacquainted. As he told me, he was accustomed. to see you going to and from school, and at the time he conceived an admiration for you which has suggested the character of the recompense which he asks."

"But surely he cannot know enough of me to be seriously interested in me. When he learns that I love another, he will dismiss this idle fancy and offer his addresses in some other quarter where they will be more acceptable."

Mr. Parker shook his head.

"I am afraid, Mabel, that whatever else he is, he is an obstinate man. So far as I can judge, his mind seems to be set upon marrying you and he will not accept anything else."

"But, father, he is probably fond of money. Offer him a large amount of money for his services—whatever he asks. Give him whatever you might otherwise intend for me—I care not for money. To me it is of no value compared with the happiness which I shall enjoy as Henry's wife. Even if you are compelled to give him half of the whole sum, the remainder will yet support you handsomely. Only, my father, do not ask me to surrender all the happiness of my life to this man's keeping."

Mabel spoke with earnestness, her cheeks glowing with the excitement of her feelings, and her face lifted imploringly to her father's, which gathered gloom as she proceeded.

"I have already suggested this to the lawyer," he said, "but without effect."

"Perhaps you did not offer him enough."

"He distinctly told me that no offer, however large, would induce him to forgo his self-named reward. Be assured, Mabel, that I desisted from no representations which would be likely to influence him. As he himself said, he might easily have concealed the whole matter from me and appropriated the whole amount to his own purposes without fear of detection, since I should be wholly ignorant of the matter."

"And why did he not? I wish that he had."

"You seem to forget, Mabel," said her father reproachfully, "that my happiness as well as yours is involved in this matter."

"Forgive me, then, my father. We are both unfortunate. We are both unhappy."

"But after all, Mabel, perhaps it will not be so bad as you imagine. He is a respectable man and, being in love with you, would no doubt treat you with great kindness and affection. We could all live together in New York and—"

"Father!" remonstrated Mabel in pained surprise. "Surely you would not recommend me to marry this man."

"I have seen more of the world than you have," said her father, half conscious and half ashamed of the selfish motives which prompted him to speak thus. "I have seen more of life and more of the world than you have, and I know that such marriages are often productive of happiness. Would it not be better to become the wife of a successful city lawyer than to spend all your life in the wilderness?"

"Father," said Mabel slowly, "you forget that I love Henry Davenport, and as for this man, I not only do not love him but, Heaven help me, I am beginning already to hate him."

"These first loves are deceptive," said Mr. Parker, still acting the part of an unworthy advocate of his own interests. "They are often mere fancies which die out with time. Take time to consider."

"Father," said Mabel, "in mercy cease. I feel that we do not understand each other. If I am to unlearn the sweet trust and confidence which I have hitherto cherished, I do not wish to live. You have asked of me too great a sacrifice, one that I cannot grant without doing wrong to my whole nature. What! shall I go to the altar with one when my heart is wholly given to another? You would not have me so recreant to myself and to God?"

"I see it is of no use to ask sympathy even from my child," said Mr. Parker peevishly.

"Father, you have my full and entire sympathy."

"That sympathy is of little worth which confines itself to words," said Mr. Parker coldly.

"But it shall not. I will see this man myself. I will kneel to him, if necessary, and beseech him to take from me the hard choice of sacrificing myself or bringing my father unhappiness."

"It will be of no use," said Mr. Parker gloomily. "Yet go it you choose. I will not attempt to control your movements."

Chapter X.

An Important Document.

Richard Clarke was seated in his room at the inn. The room he occupied was perhaps the best the rude tavern afforded, though it could hardly be considered luxurious in its appointments. In one corner stood a cot bedstead. There was a chair at each window and a small table, perhaps two feet square, between, over which hung a looking-glass of scanty dimensions, which suffered under the further disadvantage of having been fractured by some careless occupant of the room in times past. There was no wash-stand, guests being expected to perform their ablutions below. At the lawyer's special request, however, a tin washbowl had been furnished which stood on the table before mentioned, while a tin dipper supplied the place of the pitcher.

Mr. Clarke was seated on one chair while his extended limbs found a resting-place on another. A bowl of cider on the table nearby indicated that he was disposed to be convivial. A complacent smile which played over his features evinced that he was in a contented frame of mind.

"I've got him under my thumb," he soliloquized. "Thanks to my knowledge of human nature I read him at once and made up my mind how to deal with him. I can see, plainly enough, that he doesn't particularly relish having me for a son-in-law. The old fellow's pride sticks to him yet. That's unfortunate for him for it must be humbled. I have a shrewd suspicion too that the young lady won't be altogether willing to accept Dick Clarke as a substitute for that young spark of a Davenport. He seems to be quite a trim young gallant and is handsomer than I ever was. I am very glad to say that I have a proper appreciation of my own want of beauty. I remember my father used to say, 'Dick's a rough looking fellow, but he'll make his way in the world.' I mean to verify the old gentleman's prediction, if I live long enough. Let me take another look at the precious document which is, so to speak, the corner-stone of my prosperity."

Dick carefully drew from an inner pocket a letter somewhat rumpled. It was directed on the outside to Joseph Parker.

"The old gentleman would give something to get hold of this," said the lawyer complacently. "With it, he might snap his fingers at me and leave me to crawl back to my dusty office at my leisure."

He opened it and read it—for the hundredth time it may be. As however it will be new to the reader, it may be well to transcribe its contents and set before them.

It commenced as follows:

"My dear son Joseph,

Although it may prove unnecessary, yet in order to avoid all risk in the event of any unforeseen contingency such as my sudden death, I have thought proper to set down succinctly a step which I have felt it a matter of prudence to take, together with the reasons which have impelled me to take it.

"I need hardly say that through inheritance and otherwise I am the possessor of what is reckoned in these colonies a considerable fortune—amounting to not very far from twenty thousand pounds, and perhaps more. This will, in the natural course of events, descend to you, my only son. But in the present troubled state of the country (the letter bore date December, 1779) while a struggle is pending between the mother country and these colonies, the issue of which is doubtful, the security of possession is, as a matter of course, greatly endangered. It is for this reason that I have endeavored to preserve an outside neutrality, although you know that my sympathies are with England, which I trust will eventually chastise her refractory children into a return to their duty. Yet as the open avowal of these sentiments would be sure to involve me in odium, I have thought best to veil my real opinions and await passively the issue of events. Yet, as suspicions may arise, and, as so often happens in such a struggle, I may, on some pretext, be deprived of my property, I have thought it my duty to adopt some means of preserving at least a part of it to you, independent of contingency."

"What a prosy and long-winded old fellow," muttered Dick. "He might as well have come to the point in half a dozen lines. But the best part of it is to come."

He resumed the reading of the letter, and we will follow his example.

"I have, therefore, with as much secrecy as possible, realized the money value of one half of my property and at various times, as frequent as I dared, contrived to convert it into gold pieces. These I carefully laid away in a stout trunk which now lies concealed. The chief object of this communication is to reveal to you the place of concealment, that if I should be taken away during your absence the secret may not die with me.

"You will remember the small tract of land, embracing perhaps a couple of acres, at the upper part of the island on which stands the cottage of Black Phoebe, your old nurse. Being so much out of the way, I decided that this would be the best place of concealment which I could select. After some reflection, I decided not to let her into the secret, and accordingly contrived a pretext for temporary absence, during which the trunk was conveyed by night to the spot and buried at the foot of a tree. There will be no difficulty in finding the place, since as you will perhaps remember there is but this one tree on the place. It is an old apple tree, now past bearing, which stands just in the rear of the house. By my directions, a hole was dug four feet in depth at the northeast corner, and the trunk, being deposited therein, was carefully covered over, the superfluous dirt being removed so that there might be no traces left of the place having been disturbed.

"In this trunk will be found ten thousand pounds in gold,—a sum that will enable you to live comfortably and as befits your station even if you should be deprived of your remaining possessions. I trust, however, that this may not be the case, and that my precaution may prove to have been unnecessary. But however this may be, I shall feel that I have done my duty in adopting this prudent measure in your behalf.

"I am sensibly affected, dear son, when I reflect that if you are ever to read this paper, it will probably be when I am laid in the grave. Let me then speak as becomes such an occasion and counsel you to preserve unimpaired the family escutcheon which has not yet been stained by a dishonorable act. Remember that you came of a good family and have noble blood in your veins, and, so far as you are concerned, do not suffer the name to lose any of that higher consideration which has hitherto attached to it.

"In conclusion, my son, I will subscribe myself,

Your affectionate father
John Parker."

"The old gentleman little thought for whose eye he was writing," thought the lawyer. "If he had, he wouldn't have been quite so affectionate in his address—though it may turn out that I shall become, if not his son, the next thing to it. I mean his grandson."

Clarke slowly folded up the letter and replaced it in his pocket.

"I remember the old gentleman," he said musingly. "He was the very essence of respectability with his powdered hair, knee breeches, and all that. I little suspected, at that time, that I should ever stand in any near relation to him, and I fancy that it was quite as far from his thoughts. Let them talk as they may of Dame Fortune, she can do a fellow a good turn now and then and she has chosen to be kind to me. This beautiful wild flower has been growing up in the woods for me, and faith, I'll wear it."

His soliloquy was interrupted by the entrance of the landlord who thrust his head in at the door, saying, "There's a lady downstairs would like to see you, Mr. Clarke. Will you go down and see her?"

"A lady!" exclaimed the lawyer, starting from his chair in surprise. "Who is it?"

"Squire Parker's daughter."

"Mabel Parker!" returned Clarke in surprise. "I will be down directly."

Chapter XI.

An Ultimatum.

The lawyer, in spite of his frank confession of want of beauty, did not fail to pay some attention to his external appearance before going down to meet Mabel. He retied his cravat, which was awry, and, with the aid of a comb and brush, brought into somewhat better order the shock of hair which usually received little attention.

On many accounts the interview was one which Mabel dreaded. She had come to plead with a man whom she did not know to resign his claims to her hand. She could not think of him without repugnance. Perhaps indeed she might be charged with indelicacy in coming alone to see him, but she was so straight-forward and impatient of delay that she could not endure suspense and wished to bring matters to a point.

The lawyer came in with a smile that was meant to be encouraging and, bowing low, remarked, "Miss Mabel Parker, I believe."

Mabel inclined her head gravely while she answered, "You are right, sir. You are, I believe, Mr. Richard Clarke of New York."

"I am, and I may add that it affords me pleasure to make the acquaintance of one whose face has been familiar for years."

Mabel could not assure him of her own pleasure and therefore remained silent.

"This is a charming country of yours," said the lawyer complaisantly. "These green woods and beautiful meadows make me think of fairy land. I had no expectation of finding the wilderness so attractive."

"Yes, it is pleasant," said Mabel absently. She was thinking how she might introduce the subject of her errand.

"But your father appears to be better pleased with city life," remarked Clarke, glancing shrewdly at his visitor.

"You have called on my father?" said Mabel abruptly.

"I had that pleasure. What a charming situation you have."

Impatient of this irrelevant speech, and desirous of shortening the interview as far as possible, Mabel took no notice of this complimentary observation but proceeded: "He has informed me of the business which induced your coming."

"I beg you to believe that it is with the greatest qualification that I unexpectedly find it in my power to restore your father and yourself to the position for which nature designed you."

This Richard Clarke said with the air of one who was conferring a favor from the most disinterested of motives.

Mabel looked at him in surprise! "Perhaps my father misunderstood you—I hope he did—but he mentioned something about a condition."

She paused in some embarrassment.

"I did indeed name a condition, Miss Parker,—a condition which I earnestly hope you will regard with favor."

"This condition," said Mabel, determined to get through the interview as soon as possible, "this condition related to myself. You must pardon my directness, but I do not like circumlocution and wish to come to an understanding at once."

"You are quite right," said the lawyer, "and I thank you for coming to the point, and since the opportunity is afforded me, allow me to say that though this is the first occasion of my speaking with you, I have long known and admired you."

"You have the advantage of me, sir," said Mabel with reserve.

"Yet let me hope that this will not prejudice you against

me. In proposing for your hand as I did to your father, I acted from no hasty impulse but from a well-considered determination. Think that, in acceding to my request, you not only bestow happiness upon your unworthy admirer but also secure the restoration of your father and yourself to that sphere which is most congenial to you."

"As for myself," said Mabel, "I have no desire to leave the country home which I have found so attractive. I was never so happy in the city as I have been here."

Mabel did not analyze the sources of her happiness. Perhaps no one ever does so. But it is questionable whether Henry Davenport's presence would not have made the city more attractive than the country.

"Perhaps I was wrong with regard to yourself," said Clarke, bowing gallantly. "The country does indeed seem to be the fit abiding place of the flowers—more especially of the rose, the queen of flowers."

Mabel listened coldly and deigned no acknowledgement of this compliment. After pausing long enough for an answer to be made, if one was intended, the speaker went on:

"But your father—he at least would much prefer the city?"

"He would. He has never enjoyed himself much in the country and his happiness would doubtless be much promoted by a return to the scenes and acquaintances with which he was once familiar."

"It is fortunate, then, that this return is now open to him," said the lawyer, looking stealthily at his fair companion.

"And how is it open to him?" asked Mabel, fixing her eyes steadily upon the lawyer.

"By his acceptance of my offer," said Clarke, not without betraying a little confusion.

"Mr. Clarke," said Mabel, "I have come here with the intention of being entirely frank with you. The condition which you have proposed is one that it is quite impossible for my father to comply with."

"Impossible!"

"Yes, for two reasons. The first is that my father, whatever other claims he may have upon me, has no authority over my hand and its disposal. I am convinced that he does not desire to have."

"But in case of your willingness," said the lawyer eagerly.

"That is out of the question," said Mabel gravely.

"Let me hope that I may prevail upon you to alter your mind. If assiduous devotion—"

"Sir, I repeat it, this is out of the question. I will not stop to discuss the question of time and its effect upon my mind. Another circumstance stands in the way which I will not hesitate to disclose to you from motives of maidenly delicacy. Learn that my heart has been won by another, and if I marry any one, he will be my husband."

Clarke's brow darkened.

"It is young Davenport," he said.

"How you should have arrived at this knowledge, I know not," said Mabel. "However, it saves me the trouble of my intended disclosure. You are right. It is Henry Davenport."

"But," said the lawyer insinuatingly, "when he learns that your father's happiness is involved, he will agree to surrender your hand."

Mabel's face flushed indignantly. "It might occur to him," she said sarcastically, "to inquire how far such a sacrifice would promote my father's happiness. Allow me to correct an evident misapprehension. Learn, then, that my engagement to Henry Davenport is not my only obstacle to complying with the proposal you have made. The other is insurmountable."

"I do not ask you," said the lawyer, "to marry me from inclination. That will come in time and I am willing to wait for it. I am not sentimental, but I like you and want you for my wife. I am in a condition to offer your father what he values in return. You see I have stated it as a business transaction."

"I am glad you have placed it on the right footing," said Mabel. "It will make it less embarrassing. I feel free then to urge you, instead of my hand, which it is quite impossible for me to grant, to accept a part of this money which you say it is in your power to place in my father's hands."

"I have already signified to your father," said the lawyer coolly, "that this is a proposition which I cannot consider."

"Perhaps you think thus to force me to your terms," said Mabel, "but I may as well say that this is a sacrifice which I cannot make even for my father. Take money and you can name your own terms. Otherwise, you may regard business between us as at an end."

"I should prefer that you would not make up your mind too hastily," said Clarke with an incredulous look which incensed Mabel, implying as it did doubt of the strength of her resolution. "I shall remain some days more and hope during that time you may reconsider your present determination."

"Good morning, sir," said Mabel haughtily.

"What a splendid creature she is!" mused the lawyer self-complacently. "I like her all the better for her pride. She's offish now, but she'll come to it yet."

Chapter XII.

Long Arrow.

At the date of our story, some of the Indian tribes still occupied lands in the heart of our present civilization. The stern destiny which, year by year, has thrust them farther and farther away from the hunting grounds of their fathers was indeed taking shape. Already the forests had been felled, and the smoke of many a settlement rose through the clear air throughout the Eastern states, and even the eastern part of New York had become too densely peopled for the aboriginal inhabitants. It seemed impossible for the two races to breathe the same air. But in the interior of the state the settlements were so few that remnants of the tribes yet lingered, reluctant to exchange the home whose varied and beautiful scenery had so recommended it for lands farther west which were neither endeared to them by old association nor of so fair an outward aspect.

Among these remnants was a band of about fifty warriors who made their home near the beautiful lakes, of which the Empire State is justly so proud. One of their villages was located about ten miles from the settlement which has thus far been the scene of our story. It was known as Okommaka-mesit.

A space had been cleared of trees to an extent about two hundred yards square and here, scattered irregularly about, stood the wigwams of the tribe. In all, the village numbered not far from two hundred and fifty inhabitants, including men, women and children. Fortunately for the neighboring white settlement, they had always been amicably disposed to the strange race who were gaining a foothold among them. Such at least was the general sentiment, although occasionally one fiercer or gifted with greater foresight than the rest contemplated, with ill-concealed alarm and jealousy, the onward sweep of European civilization.

The chief of this tribe, or rather remnant of a tribe, bore as was usual among the Indians a name founded upon his personal qualities. The author regrets that the defective character of the Indian chronicles to which he has had access does not allow him to give this name in the original, but perhaps it may be equally edifying to supply its English meaning. The name of this chief, then, was Long Arrow, and the reader will, of course, conjecture without difficulty that the name was given in compliment to his reputation as a skilful archer. This reputation, however, rather bore reference to the past than the present, for the chief was no longer young. Sixty winters had not passed over his head without somewhat impairing, not only his bodily strength, but the accuracy of his aim, so that he no longer vaunted his present prowess but rested his fame on his ancient deeds. Yet, as was not unnatural, he still took great interest in the art in which he had once been so skilful and regarded with most favor those young men of the tribe who excelled in this department of skill.

The chief had one daughter, a maiden of sixteen who, for grace and beauty, bore off the palm among all the maidens in the village. For this reason, as well as her rank as the daughter of the leading man in the tribe, her hand was eagerly sought by more than one of the young men who surrounded her. But the daughter of a chieftain was not to be lightly or easily won. Probably Waurega herself would readily have made her own choice, but her father was not only to be consulted but expected to have a controlling voice in the matter. And Waurega, being of a yielding disposition and having a great reverence for her father, never dreamed of disputing his will.

Already he had had several applications from young men for his daughter's hand, but he had invariably answered that she was too young yet to marry. But he voluntarily promised that, on Waurega's seventeenth birthday, he should make the selection of his future son-in-law and recommended them to have patience until then.

To this advice the young men submitted with the better grace, perhaps because each one, in the plentitude either of his own vanity or his hope, fancied that his own chance of success was the best. But whether or not this should prove correct, the will of the chief was law and it was useless to think of thwarting it.

Waurega had too much of the spirit of her sex not to have some choice in the matter. Though her filial submission was such that she did not venture to mention the subject to her father, she earnestly hoped that his choice would rest upon a certain young man who bore the name of Okanoga. Waurega's preference certainly did her credit, for there was not in the village a more shapely and handsome youth than he. He was adept in all manly exercises, and had approved himself in all respects an honorable and high-minded young man and had never been charged with a base or dishonorable action.

As Waurega's seventeenth birthday approached, she could not avoid speculating much, and anxiously, upon her father's probable choice. But upon this point she was left entirely to conjecture, since, with an Indian's habitual taciturnity, he did not choose to indicate by the slightest sign what that decision would be. But upon the evening preceeding the eventful day he broke through his silence.

He had sat for an hour at the door of his lodge smoking a pipe with that imperturbable gravity which is the characteristic of an Indian. Yet occasionally his glance would stray to his daughter, who was stirring about within the lodge attending to some domestic duty. He took care, however, not to let his daughter see that she was an object of attention, for he cautiously withdrew his glance whenever he thought that she was likely to observe it.

At length, however, he removed the pipe and called his daughter by name.

"Waurega!"

At the sound of her name the maiden came instantly to her father's side and looked anxiously in his face.

"Take your seat beside me, Waurega," said the chief. "I have something for your ear."

In a grateful attitude of childlike dependence and trust, Waurega sank to the ground and rested her hand upon the knee of the chief.

"Let my father speak," she said. "His words are as music to the ear of his child."

"Thou hast ever been a good child, Waurega," said the chief, fondly stroking the luxuriant hair of his daughter.

"The heart of Waurega leaps for joy at these words from the great chief—her father," said the maiden, while her face beamed with satisfaction at this unwonted commendation from her stately and taciturn parent.

"The sight of thy face in my lodge has been very pleasing to me, and thy step has been like that of a young fawn, Waurega, but the time has come when thou must leave thy father's lodge."

The young girl murmured inaudibly and clung the closer to her parent's knees. She knew to what he referred and her heart beat faster. The next sentence, no doubt, would reveal the name of the husband whom her father had selected for her.

"Would it be Okanoga?" So she fervently hoped.

"Seventeen times the corn has ripened and the snows have fallen," said the chief, "since Waurega came to her father's lodge. She was a child then, small and weak, and her foot, now swift like the fawn's, had no power. But now she has grown into a maiden, pleasant and fair as her mother was, and the young men have asked her father to give her to them as a wife."

The chief paused, but Waurega only nestled the closer to his side and still kept silence.

"It is right that Waurega should wed," said the chief. "The Long Arrow is growing old. The young sapling has

77

become an old tree, and the time shall come when the warriors will need a new chief. It is right that Waurega should wed and raise up a successor to tread in the steps of the Long Arrow and take his place at the council-board."

"Now," thought the Indian maiden, "will my father speak the name of my husband. O that it may be Okanoga!"

But again she was mistaken.

"Waurega must be the wife of one who is brave and skilful—one whom Long Arrow shall not be ashamed to acknowledge as his son."

The old chief went on to explain the plan of selection which he had adopted. It was characteristic and showed that he had not forgotten his ancient skill with the bow.

In brief, he proposed to have a trial at archery open to all the young men in the tribe, his daughter's hand being the guerdon of the victor. The trial was to take place at ten in the morning, and immediately upon the result being known the simple rites of the Indian marriage were to take place, and Waurega would at once assume the duties of a wife.

Waurega listened in silence, and not without satisfaction, for she well knew that her favorite Okanoga was skilled in the use of the bow, and she fondly anticipated that he would win the prize.

Chapter XIII.

The Chief's Proclamation.

When the sun was an hour high, Long Arrow convoked a meeting of the young men of the tribe. There was not one who did not know the meaning of this summons, for this day had been anxiously looked forward to by more than one of the young men.

When all were assembled and silence was obtained, the chief spoke.

"My children," he said, "I have called you together to choose a husband for my daughter. For seventeen summers she has grown up in the lodge of the Long Arrow, and now she is old enough to wed. Is there any one among you who would be the husband of Waurega?"

"I! I!" shouted fifteen young men simultaneously.

The chief slowly glanced from one to another, and then his eye rested with a glance of pride upon his daughter, who stood half screened from view behind him. Despite his grave appearance he could not help feeling proud of such a tribute to the power of his daughter's attractions.

"It is well," he said after a brief pause. "There are many that would lead Waurega to their wigwam, but she can marry but one."

Again there was a pause, and the hearts of the young men beat, now high with hope, now fast with suspense.

"I cannot give her to all," continued the chief. "I would give her to the best."

Again he paused, but after a brief silence continued, his figure swelling with conscious pride.

"You know, my children, that I am called the Long Arrow. When my form was as straight and my eye as sharp as yours, there was not a young man in the tribe who could speed his arrow farther or straighter to the mark than mine. Many a time have I loosed the shaft and brought down the bird that was swift upon the wing. Many a time has my arrow drawn the heart's blood of the enemy. He that would win the daughter of Long Arrow must shoot the best arrow. I have said."

Of course it was understood that there was to be a trial of skill and that the hand of Waurega was to be the guerdon of the victor.

Two hours were allowed for the preliminary preparations. The young contestants were anxious to see that their bows were in proper trim. They at once dispersed to their respective wigwams and began to tighten the strings and select their best arrows, so that the trial might be made under the most advantageous circumstances.

Some of them had but a faint hope of success. They had been pitted against each other so many times that the particular degree of skill possessed by each was a matter of general knowledge.

Yet none wholly despaired. Accidents may happen in the best regulated families, and even the most skilful are liable to failure. There were two, however, who had hitherto borne off the palm of archery and who stood much the best chance of victory.

The first of these was Okanoga, the favored lover of Waurega. He heard the chief's proposal with satisfaction, for he had well-grounded confidence in his own skill. Besides he had everything to stimulate him to unwonted effort. He had glanced at the face of Waurega, and he interpreted aright the shy glance of encouragement. She wished for his success, and he determined to leave nothing undone to secure it.

The other, the only formidable rival of Okanoga, was the Indian introduced in the early part of this story as Indian John. It will be remembered that he served as the guide of the lawyer when wandering bewildered in the woods. His position in the tribe was by no means so desirable as that of Okanoga. He had sunk into disgrace through his habits of intoxication, which had been steadily increasing upon him. His father, with stern sorrow, lamented the degradation of his son and had often remonstrated with him, but to no purpose. John had listened sullenly, and when his father ceased speaking, would stray away by himself, and whenever by any means he obtained a sum of money or had anything to barter, it invariably found its way to the till of the landlord of Hill's Tavern.

Besides the passion for drink, there was one other to which John had yielded. In common with the other young men of the tribe he loved the chief's daughter. Till now he had loved her hopelessly, for his conduct and degradation were such that it would have been the wildest presumption for him to dream of an alliance with the pure-minded Waurega.

But now an opportunity was presented of which he might take advantage. The competition was open to all, and by the terms no one was excluded. She was without reserve to become the wife of him who shot the best arrow. John well knew his own skill and was proud of it. The time had been when in virtue of it he held a position equal to that of his chief rival Okanoga. For, among the Indians, skill and prowess universally command respect and regard. But this was before he had yielded to the baleful spirit which had brought him down from his high estate. There were times when John became sensible of his fall and formed the determination to abjure the tempting fiend which had caused it. But appetite again asserted its claims, and again he yielded.

But when the chief made the announcement which had created so great an excitement among the young men, a spark of the old fire kindled in the breast of John and his step became prouder as he thought how great a change success in the approaching trial would effect in his present position. There was nothing that would so certainly restore him to the

81

respect of his comrades, who now regarded him with ill-concealed contempt. But apart from this desirable change in the popular estimation of him, he would win the prize which so many coveted. The beautiful Waurega, daughter of the great chief, would then become his wife. He would lead her to his wigwam and henceforth become the envy of the tribe. Yes, he would try. He would do his best and perhaps, nay it was very possible that he would succeed.

The same thought had come to another. The father of John, though he had felt deeply the humiliation of his son, had not lost all confidence in him. When he came staggering home, his naturally good features wearing the besotted look of a drunkard, in all his indignation and sorrow he could not help recalling the time when John stood forth among the young men, prominent for his skill and strength, and a feeling of pride in the past mingled with his mortification for the present.

He, too, had not failed to recognize the importance of his son's seizing this moment to retrieve his well-nigh lost position and establish his reputation on its old foundation.

He waited for his son in the wigwam which they jointly occupied.

"Has my son heard the announcement of the chief?" he asked, fixing his eyes upon John.

"He has" was the brief reply.

"And does not his heart warm to the daughter of Long Arrow, the beautiful Waurega, whose step is light upon the turf and whose smile is like the sunshine?"

"Waurega is very fair. Happy will be he who shall win her to enter his wigwam," replied the son.

"Is not the arrow of John as true as that of any of the young men?" said his father persuasively, using his son's English appellation. "Does he not recall his ancient fame? Will he not strive with the young men, that perchance he may win the prize of victory? Then will the young men cease to deride him because he has given himself up to the power of the strong firewater of the English that has so often mocked him and made him appear like a silly woman. Will he not turn away from it and take the place that is his?"

"My father has spoken well," said John gravely. "I have been foolish, but now I will be wise. My arrow shall fly to the mark with those of the young men."

"It is good," said the delighted parent, who had feared that his love for drink had so far blunted the ambition of his son that he would find it difficult to lead him to his wish. "It is good. My son shall conquer. When the sun sets he shall lead the fair Waurega to his wigwam."

Cheered by this confident anticipation of his success, John sought out his bow and arrows and examined them closely to make sure that they were in a proper state to use in so important a trial.

Unfortunately for John's chances of success, a strong temptation presented itself to him while he was engaged in preparing for the trial of skill now so near at hand.

This temptation assumed a form the most difficult for one of his nature to resist.

The day previous he had succeeded in obtaining a little money for a service rendered to one of the whites, and had as a matter of course gone to the tavern to invest it in liquor. Usually he was unprovided with more than would buy what he could drink at once, but on this occasion he was better supplied. He accordingly purchased a bottle full which he brought home with him. This bottle he had laid away so that it might not meet the eye of his father. But while he was preparing for the trial, as luck would have it, the thought of this bottle, the contents of which were not more than half exhausted, came to him and with it the pangs of thirst assailed him.

Should he stop a moment and quench his thirst?

Under ordinary circumstances he would have done so, but the thought that he needed a clear head and a steady hand restrained him for a moment. He knew that, at his best, Okanoga would be a formidable rival who would not allow him to win the victory without a struggle. Should he be so imprudent as to endanger his aim by drinking, his rival's chances would be very greatly increased.

This was enough to make him pause. The thought of the magnitude of the stake for which he was playing—the attractive prize and the restoration to respectability—might well lead him to struggle with his craving appetite.

But inclination is never without its sophistries. After some vacillation of purpose John argued to himself that a small draught would make no difference. It might even increase his chances of success by making him feel more lively and animated.

At any rate he was resolved to test it, and accordingly laid down his bow and arrows and made his way to the hiding-place where he had laid the bottle.

It proved to be more than half full. John's eyes sparkled as he held it up to the light, and from that moment he resigned himself without a struggle to the power of his enslaver. He had indeed intended to drink only a little, but it was impossible for him to control his appetite once aroused. Tipping it up, he drank and drank until the bottle was empty. Then, overcome by the strength of his potations, he sank down in a stupor with the bottle by his side.

Leaving him in this condition, we shift the scene and conduct the reader to the spot where the trial is to take place.

The village of Okommakamesit was located in an open space in the centre of which were situated the buildings. Around these was a belt of land, a part of which was devoted to the limited agricultural purposes for which the Indian requires it. On one side, however, it was unplanted. It was here that the trial in archery was to take place.

Of course, so important an event made a great stir in the little settlement. In an Indian village even more than in a small New England town, everything of private interest becomes common property. This arises in a great measure from their living so much in common. Of course, therefore, such an occurrence as a trial which should decide to whom the chief's daughter should be given was no ordinary one.

Half an hour before the time arrived, the people of the village—men, women and children—were gathered in groups at the spot where it was understood that it would take place. All the village were collected except the young braves who were to contend for the prize. They were busily engaged in testing their bows and fitting them for service. Among the exceptions, also, were the chief whose dignity as well as his own interest in the result made it only proper that he should remain away. Last, but not least, Waurega herself, the fair subject of all these preparations, was concealed from view in her father's lodge. To her it was a momentous time. An hour would decide her destiny for life. She entertained a well-grounded hope that Okanoga would prove successful, but this was not certain. His bow might break, his arrow might be too light or too heavy, perhaps even the knowledge of the importance of the contest might act unfavorably upon him by depriving him of the coolness which such a trial eminently required. Besides, she had accidentally learned that John was about to enter the lists, and she knew too well his ancient skill not to have some apprehensions on this score. There was not one of the contestants whom she would not sooner have succeed than he. If she had not known her father so well, she might have thought that in such an event he would draw back from his engagement. But this was impossible. Long Arrow was a man of his word and would keep it at all hazards. No doubt it would be exceedingly distasteful to him to give his daughter to one who had so degraded himself in the estimation of the tribe, but it would be done.

Waurega, then, had some reason to feel disturbed. Her life destiny was about to be settled and, hardest of all, she must remain passive while it was being decided. There was nothing which she could do to ensure the victory to the lover of her choice, otherwise than to let him know how ardently she longed for his success, and of this he was already well aware.

But the minutes were flying and the limited time allowed

to the contestants for preparation had nearly passed. As Waurega sat with downcast eyes, her mind given up to anxious speculations upon the uncertainties of her position, suddenly her father presented himself.

He was dressed in the style which he was wont to adopt on occasions of importance, and was resolved that no effort should be spared on his part to impart dignity and impressiveness to the approaching spectacle.

"Is my daughter ready to go forth and see the young men strive which shall lead her to his wigwam?"

"Need Waurega go?" asked the maiden with an appealing glance. She felt that she would prefer to remain by herself until the issue was decided and thus be spared the anxiety of watching the varying success of the different claimants for her hand. But this was evidently no part of her father's intention. He considered that it would not be in consonance with the proprieties of the occasion (and it is a mistake to think that the Indians and others whom we are wont to consider more unconventional than ourselves are really less wedded to the conventions which prevail among them than ourselves).

To Waurega's appeal, therefore, the chief answered by intimating in a manner which could not be mistaken that it was not only his desire but his will that she should be present on the occasion.

Trained up to habits of implicit obedience, Waurega never thought of questioning the decision of her father but at once proceeded to array herself for the occasion. And here, as was not unnatural under the circumstances, a little of that admiration for finery and a desire to appear as well as possible in the eyes of her rustic admirers led Waurega to array herself in her best attire. She knew that she would be a general centre of observation to all who were present, and she reflected with a little complacency how much envy she would excite in the bosoms of some maidens in the tribe who felt themselves fortunate if they could secure but a single lover.

Waurega's dress would not perhaps have excited much

complacency in a belle of the present day. She had, at some time, become the possessor of a piece of bright red calico, obtained from the English settlement nearby, which she had fashioned into a garment to suit her own taste. Around her neck she wore two separate strings of beads of different colors. Of these she was not a little proud, viewing them in the same light as a fashionable lady would her diamonds. Other parts of her attire must be left to the imagination of the reader. It is enough to say that when she presented herself to her father and professed herself ready to go forth, he viewed her with a critical look which subsided into a glance of approbation. Moreover, the thoughts which she had expended upon her dress had superseded for a time the more anxious thoughts which the occasion was calculated to inspire.

Chapter XIV.

The Trial of Skill.

The young men who were to engage in the trial of skill were already on the ground. On a similar occasion among the whites, there would doubtless have been a large amount of noise and confusion, but here, on the contrary, the most perfect decorum reigned.

The rival archers formed a group by themselves. Whatever might have been their feelings towards each other, in reference to the approaching contest nothing appeared in their faces but that impassive look with which an Indian so successfully veils his real thoughts.

When, however, Long Arrow, the chief, led out Waurega, attired in her Indian finery, nature asserted itself and a low murmur of admiration ran along the whole line. But this was immediately checked and their attention was at once called to the purpose for which they had assembled.

For a mark, a circular section of bark had been stripped from a tree at the distance of a hundred yards. In removing the bark, however, an inner ring had been left and, while an arrow striking anywhere within the circle would indicate fair skill, it was expected that the best archers would hit within the inner ring in which the exact centre had been marked as nearly as could be indicated. To hit this, at such a distance, would require a degree of skill which might well entitle the one who displayed it to the glory and meed of victor.

All stood by, waiting for the chief to give the signal for the trial to commence.

Raising his hand to command attention he commenced:

"My children, you have come to see which can draw the best bow. The daughter of Long Arrow is before you." Here he pointed to Waurega, who modestly cast down her eyes.

The chief proceeded to reiterate his assurance of the morning that he who came out of the approaching contest a victor should lead Waurega to his wigwam as his wife.

The signal to commence was now given and, according to previous arrangement, one of the number stepped forward and drawing his bow to the proper position let fly the arrow.

The young man who had been appointed to lead off was of a character more frequently found among the whites than among his own nation. In other words, he had a great deal of self-complacency with a very little real merit on which to base it.

True to his character, he stepped up to the place appointed with the step of one that was confident of victory, and after a sweeping glance around him to see if he was likely to receive the attention which he coveted, he threw himself into an attitude and, after sundry preliminary flourishes, discharged his arrow as above described.

The eyes of the spectators simultaneously followed the flight of the arrow, and a laugh of derision was heard on all sides when it was found that instead of hitting the centre, as the archer had boasted that he should do, it had not even struck the tree.

This utter lack of success was too much even for the self-complacent youth who had drawn the bow. He slunk back to his former place, muttering something to the effect that his bow was not in good condition.

He was quickly succeeded by the next contestant, who, taught by the humiliating failure of his predecessor that it was not well to put on airs, walked up modestly and drew his bow with caution. His shot was a very good one, striking the inner circle of bark which had been left as above described.

The youth left the stand well pleased with his success. He did not anticipate gaining the prize, for he well knew that there were others present who were his superior. But he had exhibited a very commendable degree of skill and had no reason to be ashamed of his effort.

To him succeeded another, a mere youth, who had as yet attained but the age of eighteen and who, by courtesy alone, was admitted to the present contest. His youth precluded him from being a claimant for Waurega's hand, but he wished to have a part in the trial in order to measure his skill with that of the rest.

His arrow struck within the outer circle towards the rim. This too, considering the inexperience of the archer, was a creditable shot.

But it is not my purpose to narrate in detail the efforts of the contestants. The first proved to be the poorest. All struck the tree, though one failed to strike within the circle. At length but one remained, and this Okanoga, who by general consent had been suffered to take the last place. Great as was his skill, the task which remained for him was not of the easiest. Two of those who had preceded him had struck within the inner circle, one very near the centre. The success of the last had struck Waurega with sudden terror. Her own training had taught her that the shot was an admirable one. What increased her apprehension was the personal dislike which she entertained towards the one thus successful.

It was with a glance unconsciously appealing that she looked at Okanoga as he approached the stand.

The young man's air was cool and composed. His step was elastic and he did not appear to fear for the result. He appeared strikingly handsome as he stood in an attitude of careless grace, with one foot placed a little before the other. More than Waurega looked upon him as the Adonis of the tribe, and more than one would have been glad to win him from the chief's daughter. So among the maidens it was generally hoped that he would be unsuccessful in the present trial, as he would then be obliged to seek another bride. The men in the tribe, except those personally interested, were, on the contrary, hopeful of his success. But all, whatever might be their feelings, watched with the greatest interest the appearance of this last champion whose good or ill success would decide the question.

Though not flustered, Okanoga evidently felt the responsibility of his position. With a fair reliance upon his own ability, he was by no means inclined to a rash confidence. He therefore exercised the utmost care in taking aim. With his keen eye he fixed upon the central spot and aimed for that. His arrow was discharged amid the greatest excitement on the part of the spectators. A moment of suspense and, quickly cleaving the air, it struck and quivered in the centre.

There was a loud murmur of applause in which even some of the disappointed joined. They applauded the shot rather than the archer. When the question was thus settled, Okanoga drew aside, and lifting his eyes to the face of the chief, modestly waited for him to speak.

By a gesture the chief signified to the young man to advance.

He took the hand of his unresisting daughter and said, "I have seen the bow of Okanoga and it is strong. I marked the flight of his arrow and it was swift. It struck the mark. Okanoga's arrow is the best. Let him lead the daughter of the chief to his wigwam."

The heart of Okanoga beat high with exultation and his eye sparkled with joy as he took the proffered hand and led away the embarrassed but happy Waurega.

Meantime, a different scene was enacting in another cabin.

John had not made his appearance among the contestants. His father's eye scanned anxiously the ranks of the young men and he could not see him. His heart sank within him, for he had set his heart upon his son's embracing this chance of winning back his lost reputation.

It occurred to him, however, that he might be preparing his bow. But when one after another stepped up and discharged his arrow, the father became uneasy and stole away from the crowd, taking his way to his own wigwam.

He had scarcely entered when the cause of his son's

absence was revealed to him. Prostrate, he lay upon the floor in the stupor of intoxication with the bottle at his side.

A stern anguish settled upon the face of the father, but without disturbing his son he went back to the scene of the contest and watched the remainder of the proceedings, outwardly calm but with an aching heart.

But during this time he had taken his resolution, which he only waited for the conclusion of the trial to carry into execution.

Chapter XV.

The Father's Conflict.

The iron had entered deeply into the soul of the shamed and indignant father. In proportion as he had been proud of the skill and promise of his son, he felt a like sorrow at the bitter disappointment of his most cherished hopes. He remembered the fondness with which he had watched the youthful gambols of his child—dearer to him because his only son, his first and last born. He remembered how, even then, he felt proud of the boy's superiority to his playfellows and looked forward with hope to his assuming, by right of merit, a place in the tribe second only to that of the chief. There came back to him a hundred trifles—yet no trifles in a father's remembrance—on which he had dwelt fondly when his son was yet in the freshness of his untainted youth, ere he had bowed his knee to the idol which the whites had set up to lure their people to destruction.

Even after he began to develop the fatal taste which had become so strong, he hoped for the best—that his son would break away from the unworthy habit which was sapping the foundations of his manhood and once more walk erect in all the consciousness of his strength and superiority over his fellows.

But now these hopes were forever at an end. John had resisted the strongest inducement which could possibly be brought to bear upon him. He had had it in his power at one bound to vault back into his wonted place. Reputation and affection alike combined to bid him put under his feet the serpent which enthralled him. But, notwithstanding all these motives to conquer his appetite, if only for a short time, he had ignominiously fallen a victim to the bottle. The father felt that this decided the matter. After this, his son's reformation was no longer to be hoped. For the remainder of his life he was destined to wear the degrading chains of the enslaver, bringing disgrace upon himself, upon his father, and upon his tribe.

This thought was bitter in the extreme to the proud old man. A spirit akin to that of the Roman father rose in his heart, and he resolved to take a step which only utter despair could prompt—that he would take away that life which, if spared, would be spent in such humiliating subjection. No longer should the smile of derision appear on the faces even of the children when his son staggered home in helpless inebriety. It would be a grievous thing to be childless by his own act, but he saw no alternative. He did not stop to regard the consequences to himself. Probably they would not be serious, parental authority being greater among the Indians than with the whites, and he would be regarded as having acted not without some provocation. But even if the act were to be followed by his own death, this consideration would not have stayed his hand. He was an Indian and had all the Indian contempt of death. The assertion and protection of his own honor he looked upon as of much more moment that the question of life.

Long did the father ponder in bitterness of soul on his son's degradation before he came to this resolution. Having formed it, he took his way slowly to his lodge where he found his son, as when he last saw him, lying upon the earthen floor with the bottle beside him. His eyes were closed, and his stupor was not yet over.

The father gave one glance at him and then walked to the corner where he was accustomed to keep his tomahawk.

He lifted it and stood for a moment gazing thoughtfully upon it. To him it brought back a thousand recollections of incidents in the field and in the warpath. With it he had cleft the skull of a chief of the Seminoles, and many a less noted foe had bitten the dust under its vengeful blows. By it, he had won all this fame as a doughty warrior. But now his step had become slow and his eye had lost its wonted keenness. His arm retained a portion, only, of its ancient strength. He was one of the old men now, and would go forth no more on the warpath. His tomahawk had been laid aside and he had thought to use it no more. The time was when he had intended to bequeath it to his son, telling him at the same time of the brave execution which it had wrought and exhorting him not to fall behind his father's fame. But the time for such thought was over. His son had proved recreant. He had tarnished his father's honorable fame, and he had reserved it as the last and crowning work of this his trusty companion in a hundred skirmishes to put an end to the life of his son.

The old man lifted the weapon, stained with the blood which it had drunk, and strode to the side of his son.

He had thought his resolution firm, but as he looked down upon the form at his feet, his stern purpose wavered.

The face of his son assumed to him, it might have been his indignation preternaturally active at that time which suggested it, but he fancied he saw a startling resemblance in the expression to the mother, now for ten years dead, and whom he had loved with an intensity not common among his people.

Then the thought arose:—"It was her son as well as his that he was about to slay. When they met in the happy hunting-grounds, would she not reproach him?" This thought called up others which appealed to the natural tenderness with which he had once regarded his only child, and which in spite of the latter's shortcomings was only slumbering and not wholly lost.

Twice he raised the tomahawk, and twice he let his arm fall to his side, his resolution each time giving way.

It was at this moment that John opened his eyes.

He was so far recovered from the effects of his intoxication as to regard with astonishment the aspect and attitude of his father.

"What would my father do?" he asked, hardly comprehending the real purpose of his father.

"What has his son done?" demanded the father bitterly. "Has he not brought shame to the lodge of his father and made himself to be laughed at by the women and the boys?"

"Who laughs at John?" demanded the young man with a touch of his ancient fierceness. "Show him to me, and my knife shall drink his blood."

The father laughed, a bitter, mocking laugh.

"John has sold himself to the English for their firewater. He is no longer a man. He has become a woman. Once he could shoot, but he can do so no more. All the young men shoot better than he."

"It is a lie," said the son fiercely.

Strangely enough the father seemed to look with stern joy upon these ebullitions of his son's anger. Had he meekly acquiesced in the reproaches, his heart would have hardened against him and he might yet have carried out his purpose. But he recognized in the young man's impatience a remnant of the ancient spirit which he feared had died out in his heart.

He continued: "The young men tried their bows to see which should shoot the best arrow and lead the daughter of the chief to his wigwam. All the young men were there, but John was not there. He did not dare to shoot with the young men, for he is not a warrior, he is only a dog."

The breath of the young man came fast, and he glared at his father with a look of determined hostility.

"John is not a dog. He is a great brave," he muttered sullenly.

His father laughed in derision.

"He is a dog—a drunken dog," he reiterated. "Let him go and live among dogs. The lodge of his father is no longer for him. His father casts him out—this tribe cast him out. Let him go where he will."

96

The young man cast an anguished look at his father. This was a measure which he had not contemplated. To be cast out in this way was the deepest humiliation.

"Does my father mean what he says?" he asked, unwilling to believe without further confirmation what had just been uttered.

"He is a father no longer—he has no son, for his son has become a stranger to him."

John heard this sentence of banishment with feelings of dismay and grief, but he was too proud to expostulate with his father or seek a reversal of the sentence. With that proud resignation which is characteristic of an Indian he merely replied: "It is good. John has no father."

Then, staggering to his feet, he left the wigwam with a gait slightly unsteady and without looking back took his way to the forest.

His father looked after him with an anguished spirit, and a feeling of loneliness and desolation settled down upon him. But he was glad that he had not obeyed his first impulse and taken his son's life.

Chapter XVI.

The lawyer is put under bonds.

When John left his father's wigwam, he well understood that the sentence which had been passed upon him was no mere impulsive act upon his father's part which might be revoked at the end of a few hours, but was final. Henceforth he was left to shift for himself. He must make up his mind what course to pursue. He could not hope to rejoin his tribe. They would undoubtedly sustain his father in the course which he had adopted. Besides, in spite of his degradation, he had too much pride to wish reconciliation on terms which would no doubt involve humiliation to himself.

So far as the supply of his necessities was concerned, he felt no alarm. He had his bow and arrows with him, and the woods would supply him with game.

As he had eaten nothing since morning, he felt the necessity of immediately looking out for some game. He had now so far recovered from the effects of his potation that he could trust himself to shoot without the apprehension of failing from an unsteady hand.

As if in answer to the call of his necessity, a noble deer sped by him not five minutes after he had commenced looking about him.

With the rapidity of one accustomed to the use of the bow, John adjusted the arrow with celerity and sped it on its death-dealing way. The hunter's aim was unerring. The shaft overtook and brought low the noble game.

The Indian was advancing on his prey when a sharp sound was heard and a convulsive movement of the deer testified that a second weapon had done its work. He was at once the victim of the Indian bow and the European musket.

A moment afterwards, and the one who had discharged the musket came through the bushes.

It proved to be Clarke the lawyer, who was spending the time which he was compelled to wait for the expected favorable decision from Mabel in such recreation as the woods afforded.

He had considered it a piece of great good luck when he got upon the track of the deer, never having had the good luck to shoot one and being desirous of bearing it home as a trophy.

He had not suspected the agency of the Indian in the death of the deer till, on making his appearance, he found John kneeling beside it as it lay in its last gasp at the foot of a tree.

"Hallo!" he exclaimed. "It appears to me, my good friend, that you are making pretty free with my game."

The Indian looked up in surprise, but did not offer to stir from his place.

"Don't you understand me? I tell you that the animal is mine—the victim of my bow and spear, as the Scriptures have it."

In reply, the Indian pointed significantly to his arrow which he had just drawn from the deer, as was evident from the blood which still adhered to it.

"You smeared it with blood from the musket wound," said Clarke suspiciously.

"John shot it—here," said the Indian, pointing out the place where his arrow had struck and penetrated the deer.

"Zounds," said the lawyer chopfallen. "I don't know but you did have a share in it, but don't you see that wound would never have killed the deer. You would have lost it after all, if my musket-ball had not come in to finish the work."

John, who understood the drift of this remark, evidently did not assent to the lawyer's view, but still insisted that the deer was lawfully his.

Clarke had no especial use for the deer. It had no value to him beyond furnishing an evidence of his success as a sportsman. It was only natural for him to be proud of his first game, and he had imagined for himself quite a triumph in carrying it into the village. But John's claim interfered fatally with his intention. Though he might plume himself on killing the deer, there was no especial glory in being its joint slayer, especially when, as John contended, it had already been brought to the ground when he fired at it. To urge a claim under such circumstances, if known, would only subject him to ridicule, as he could very well imagine.

In this state of things it occurred to him to effect a compromise with the Indian, which he thought he might readily do by the judicious use of a little money.

So he broached the subject by saying, "Come, John, you don't want this deer."

The Indian asserted doggedly that it was rightfully his and that he would have it.

"But," urged the wily lawyer, "if you will let me have it, and I admit that it is yours, I will give you some silver which will be worth a great deal more to you than the deer."

This was an argument which the Indian understood. He had already learned the use of money by his intercourse with the whites. He knew that his favorite drink could be obtained on more favorable terms for this than in the way of barter, and as this was the destination of the deer he might as well accept the white man's proffer.

"How much?" he asked sententiously.

The lawyer drew out his wallet and opening it took out a silver dollar.

This he held up in his hand and showing it to John said: "You shall have this if you will let me have the deer and say nothing of having shot it. That is an indispensable condition. Do you agree?"

But the lawyer had, in his eagerness, committed an error, from which the caution taught by his profession ought to have saved him.

In opening his pocket-book, he incautiously displayed a part of the contents. These included a number of gold pieces which were plainly revealed to the Indian. Now John was so far versed in the usages of the whites as to be aware of the greatly superior value of gold to silver. Here was a strong temptation for him. He knew that the gold which he saw would buy him many gallons of rum. It might keep him supplied for months. Besides this it would buy him a lodging or a dinner whenever he chose. It could hardly be said that he was little bound by moral considerations touching the abstract rectitude or iniquity of the act by which, if at all, he must become possessed of the object which he coveted.

While Clarke was holding out the dollar to tempt him to the bargain, the Indian was rapidly making up his mind what to do.

By a sudden and on the lawyer's part wholly unforeseen movement, he snatched the pocket-book from his grasp, pinioned his arms with one of his own, and drawing forth a strong cord, proceeded to tie him hand and foot.

Of course, this was not effected without resistance. But the lawyer was no match in strength for the athletic young Indian. Besides, he was taken suddenly and at a disadvantage. There was one weapon of offense which he freely used, however, and that was his tongue. He berated the Indian in the most forcible terms with which his vocabulary could supply him, and among these were some which it may be advisable not to transfer to these pages.

But for words the Indian cared not. He proceeded swiftly and dexterously in his task, and in the space of a minute the lawyer was lying bound hand and foot, side by side with the booty which he coveted.

Having possessed himself of the pocket-book, John paid no regard to the deer but went on his way, leaving the lawyer almost speechless with rage and vexation.

"What a cursed fool I was to show him the pocket-book!" he muttered, vexed with his own imprudence, which he called to mind when it was too late. "I deserve all this.

There were over a hundred dollars in that pocket-book, and good Heavens!" the lawyer started in affright as this new misfortune flashed upon him, "good Heavens! only this morning I put into it that fatal letter. If, by any chance, it should fall into the hands of the Parkers or young Davenport, my fortune is lost beyond redemption. That cursed Indian! I could shoot him with a good relish. If I could only free myself from these cords!"

The lawyer little suspected to what angel of consolation he was to be indebted for his release from bonds.

Chapter XVII.

Zack's Discovery.

In snatching the lawyer's pocket-book, John had acted from a sudden impulse. He understood that his daring outrage would compel him to leave the neighborhood, but for this he cared little. In fact, this was a step on which he had already determined and would require no sacrifice on his part. It would be disagreeable after a formal expulsion to meet the members of his own tribe as he must do if he continued to roam these woods.

When he had placed a half mile between himself and his victim who lay writhing in his bonds, he opened the pocket-book and with some curiosity began to examine the contents.

These consisted of the gold already mentioned, a small sum in silver, and various papers.

Among these was the note which conveyed the valuable information relating to the Hidden Treasure!

John took out the gold and silver and deposited them in his own pouch. The papers he very evidently held of very little account, for with a contemptuous gesture he took them out and threw them upon the ground. His attire not supplying him with that convenient receptacle a pocket, he threw down the pocket-book also, and then, with a self-satisfied look, he turned his face to the north.

It so happened that our young friend Zack, whose disposition to roam about was much greater than his love for books, was searching for squirrels in that part of the woods and, some fifteen minutes after the Indian had taken his departure, came to the tree under which were strewn the pocket-book and the papers which it had contained.

At sight of the pocket-book Zack's eyes glistened, and he pounced upon it as an eagle upon his prey.

"Well, I'm in luck this time," he thought. "What a jolly thing it is to find a pocket-book. I wonder whether there's much in it."

By this time he had opened it and discovered its emptiness.

"Plague take it! It's just my luck!" he exclaimed with a gesture of disappointment. "I might have known there wouldn't be any money in any pocket-book I'd find. I wonder who it belongs to. O, here's his name—Richard Clarke. It's that man that's boarding up to Hill's Tavern. I wonder who's been afoul of him."

Here Zack spied the papers lying upon the grass and, with a boy's curiosity, took them up and began to examine them.

Generally they were of little interest, but the last which he took up he read with more and more attention, until when he had completed the perusal he exclaimed, slapping his knee, "Well, if that Clarke isn't a rascal! I knew he was 'round here for some mischief. Here's a letter that belongs of right to the Squire. I thought there was something in the wind by the Squire's glum looks and Mabel's looking so worried. Shouldn't wonder if this fellow wanted to marry Mabel for her money and was meaning to keep this secret till he's got it all arranged."

Without any clue beyond his own observation, Zack had unwittingly hit upon the truth of the matter, or at least in the neighborhood of the truth.

He was aroused from his meditation by a voice accosting him in this wise.

"Well, Zack, what are you meditating about this morning? You seem to be wrapt in thought."

"O, is it you, Mr. Davenport?" said Zack starting. "I—I thought it might be that fellow down to the tavern."

The young man's expression changed, for he had been made acquainted by Mabel with the nature of Clarke's expectations and was not disposed to feel very friendly towards his rival.

"That man is a rascal, Zack!" said he briefly.

"Don't I know it!" said Zack confidently.

"What do you know about it?" asked young Davenport, a little surprised that Mabel should have made a confidant of the good-hearted but rather rattle-pated youth before him.

Thinking there might be something which he did not know and desirous of verifying the truth or falsity of his suspicions, Zack began to show reserve, and thrusting the important paper slyly into his breast pocket, answered: "Well, I don't know as I know all that's going on, but I know something that you and Miss Mabel and the Squire, too, would be glad to know."

"Ha!" said Henry Davenport eagerly. "What is it? Tell me at once."

But Zack was too old a bird to be so quickly caught.

"After all," said he meditatively, "I can't tell whether you will care much for it unless I know the circumstances about this fellow over to the tavern."

"Pshaw, Zack!" said Davenport impatiently, "it wouldn't interest you much. Just tell me what it is that you have found out."

"I guess," said Zack shrewdly, "that what I've found out wouldn't interest you much, so I guess I won't say anything about it."

"I see," said the young man, "that you are a sharp boy, and I must give up to you. You must know, then, that Mabel and myself have made up our minds to—to—"

"Hitch teams," suggested Zack, with an intelligent nod.

"Well, perhaps that will express it," said the young man smiling, "but unfortunately for my purpose this lawyer Clarke—"

"He's a lawyer, is he?" said Zack. "Well, I reckoned he was."

105

"—has the presumption to aspire to Mabel's hand also . . ."

"Why don't she tell him to clear out and go about his business?"

"Unfortunately, he has in his possession a secret of a most important character, which he uses to influence the mind of Mr. Parker, who is so discomposed thereby that Mabel is also made unhappy."

"You don't happen to know what the secret is about?" said Zack in a very suggestive tone.

"I see, Zack, you will allow no half-way confidences," said young Davenport laughing. "I might as well be frank and tell you the whole. It appears, then, that Mr. Parker inherited only half of his father's property. That, as you know, he lost through his misfortunes in business."

"What became of the rest?" questioned Zack, who of course knew all about it but for certain reasons of his own desired to hear how much the young man knew about it.

"That is just what *we* don't know and this fellow does. We only know that Mr. Parker's father was afraid his property would be taken away from him during the war, and accordingly converted half of his wealth into gold and concealed it. He left a letter behind, disclosing the place of concealment, but this letter his son never received or even saw. By some unlucky accident it fell into the hands of this fellow Clarke, who keeps it to himself and uses it with Mr. Parker as a means of obtaining his consent to wed Mabel."

"How much money was there?" asked Zack.

"Fifty thousand dollars!"

"Crackey! that would make a pile, wouldn't it? I say it would be worth something to get hold of that letter."

"Yes, I would give something if I could set eyes on it."

"You would?" said Zack.

"Of course I would. But how queerly you act this morning. What have you been taking?"

"A little—exercise," said Zack demurely. "But say, how much would you give?"

106

"Five hundred dollars!" said the young man, more for the sake of satisfying Zack with an answer than from any other reason.

"Then, old fellow, I guess I'll take it now," said the boy, pulling out the paper from its place of concealment.

"What's that?" demanded Henry Davenport in surprise.

"Just read it, and I guess you'll find it all right," said Zack.

It was read with emotions of joyful surprise.

"Zack, you're an angel of good tidings!" he exclaimed, clasping the boy's hand warmly in his.

"Thank you for your favorable opinion," said Zack, his eyes sparkling with merriment. "I'm rather badly off for wings, considering I'm an angel, and I guess you'd better let me have the money so that I can buy a new pair."

His companion laughed.

"I won't forget you, Zack," he said, "but let us go to the house and tell Mabel and her father of this welcome discovery."

Chapter XVIII.

The Fair Deliverer.

Nothing could well be imagined more aggravating than the lawyer's situation. To be upon the ground in a cramped position, with the limbs confined by a strong cord, can hardly be considered agreeable. But when you add to this that the prospect of deliverance is very uncertain, and that while so confined future plans of advantage are in imminent danger of being knocked in the head, it may well be conceived that there are other situations which may be considered preferable.

Such as I have described was the position of the lawyer.

"That cursed Indian!" he exclaimed, smarting with the pain of the cord. "I could shoot him with a good relish. If he had only left me the papers, I wouldn't have minded the money so much, but it is torture to lie here not knowing how much mischief he may do me."

After a time he became less desponding and reflected that after all things were not quite as bad as they might have been. The mere possession of the paper was nothing to him. It was only important that it should not fall into the hands of others who might make use of it, and especially of those to whom it rightfully belonged. Now the presumption was that John, who did not know how to read, would destroy the papers contained in the pocket-book as of no value to himself and as likely, if discovered in his possession, to bring him into trouble. If he destroyed them, well and good—no evil would result to the lawyer and the secret would still be his.

Clarke, who was of a sanguine temperament, gradually worked himself into the conviction that this was what was most likely to happen. Thus his trouble of mind was somewhat diminished, although his bodily discomfort remained. But his deliverer, although he knew it not, was even now at hand.

Not to protract the reader's suspense, let me say that Mehitable had come out into the woods in search of some peculiar kind of herb which was a sovereign remedy for rheumatism, from the ruthless attacks of which she sometimes suffered.

The spinster had, from the first, been favorably impressed with the lawyer's appearance. She had indulged a hope that his opinion of herself was not less favorable. She had observed nothing likely to lead her to suppose that Mabel was the object of his attentions. Besides, she knew that an attachment existed between Henry Davenport and her young mistress, and this was sufficient to prevent her imagining that the lawyer's stay in the village had anything to do with her.

This delusion of hers was encouraged by Zack, who, in a spirit of roguery, enjoyed the affected bashfulness and confusion assumed by Mehitable when spoken to on the subject. By his continued teasing, he had done much to keep alive in her the hope that her destiny was at hand and that ere long she would return to New York with the lawyer as his bride.

In fact, it was with this pleasing subject that Mehitable's thoughts were occupied when chance led her to the immediate neighborhood of the prisoner.

His quick eyes detected her approach, and recognizing her at once he called out, "Mehitable!"

"Who calls me?" asked the spinster in a voice tremulous with affright, for it was the fear of her life that the Indians would someday carry her off, though it would be hard to tell what object they could have in the abduction.

Afraid that she would leave him in her alarm and so

deprive him of the present chance of escape, the lawyer cried, "Don't be afraid. It is only I, Richard Clarke, the lawyer. Surely you know me!"

For the first time discovering her supposed lover and his situation, Mehitable clasped her hands, and feeling that the words would be excused in her surprise, exclaimed, "Dear, dear Mr. Clarke, how came you so cruelly tied?"

"It was that cursed Indian," said the lawyer sullenly.

"Is the Injun here?" asked Mehitable, showing a disposition to fly. "I don't dare to stay. I shall be carried off and made to marry one of the copper colored wretches. Oh, oh!"

"I don't think you need be alarmed on that score," said Clarke a little dryly. "Besides there are none near. It was only one that overpowered me, and he would not have succeeded if he had not taken me unexpectedly. It was the rascal who goes by the name of Indian John."

"I'd like to tear his eyes out," said Mehitable with proper indignation.

"You had better untie these cords," said the lawyer, not appreciating her warm advocacy of his cause.

Mehitable stooped down, and with the coy look of a young girl essayed to unloose the fastenings. But, on a sudden, when she had about half completed her task, she stopped short and looked unutterably bashful.

"What's the matter? Can't you untie it?" asked Clarke.

"It wasn't that," said Mehitable.

"What was it, then? I wish you'd be kind enough to make haste, for it is rather painful feeling the strain of these cords."

"I—I was thinking that we were alone," said Mehitable bashfully.

"And suppose we were—what then?" inquired Clarke in great surprise.

"I was thinking that if I untied you, you might go and—and—being a great deal stronger than I am—might go and kiss me, and I couldn't help myself."

"Can anything exceed the folly of this ridiculous old

110

maid?" thought Clarke impatiently. "I must even humor her folly."

"But I promise you on my honor," he said emphatically, "that you have nothing to fear from me."

Mehitable would have been better pleased with some gallant demonstration, but was determined not to yield the point yet.

"And you'll excuse me for calling you 'dear Mr. Clarke'?" she said, veiling her face with her handkerchief.

"I didn't hear you call me so."

"But I did," said Mehitable candidly. "It was in the surprise of first beholding you in this distressed condition that I addressed you in that manner. You won't take advantage of it, will you, Mr. Clarke?"

The lawyer assured her very emphatically that she had nothing whatever to fear from him and urged her to complete the work of his deliverance.

This she at length did, but, while doing so, favored him with some reminiscences of the lover whom she had rejected and who in consequence, as she darkly intimated, had found existence too grievous a burden to bear.

"Then why didn't you marry him?" asked Clarke bluntly.

"Because I could not give him the gushing affections of my young and unsophisticated heart," said Mehitable sentimentally. "I have since seen those—that is, I have seen one whom I think I might learn to love."

"Indeed, who is it?"

"Do not ask me, Mr. Clarke. It is a secret which I can never speak to the ear of anyone, least of all to you."

"And why not to me?" demanded the lawyer.

"Because—O, Mr. Clarke, do not ask me any more questions, for I might reveal the state of my heart, and indeed I must not."

"Zounds, if I don't believe she's in love with me," said Clarke to himself. "In that case I certainly won't press the old girl to make what might prove to be rather an awkward revelation."

"Won't you come to the house?" asked Mehitable.

"Thank you," said Clarke, "I shall not be able to do so just now. I must follow on the track of that confounded Indian, who has served me such a miserable trick."

"O, don't!" exclaimed Mehitable, clasping her hands. "For my sake don't! He will kill and scalp you, and I—we all should miss you so much."

"Thank you," said Clarke, slightly smiling, "but I apprehend no danger—I shall now be on my guard. I am much obliged to you for acting as my deliverer, and must now bid you good morning."

"I wonder if he loves me!" thought the spinster. "What a beautiful man he is. I don't know but it is my duty to marry him if he asks me. If I can see that it is my duty I will submit without a murmur."

There was abundant reason to believe that this statement was correct.

Meanwhile, Clarke searched until he found the pocketbook lying in the path. There were no papers to be seen, Zack having carried away the whole.

"The Indian has undoubtedly destroyed them," thought Clarke. "In that case matters are not so bad as they might be."

Chapter XIX.

A Fit of Melancholy.

Mr. Parker was not a man of strong mind or strong feelings. When he was angry or disturbed, instead of blazing out in a sudden fit of passion, he indulged himself and annoyed others by a fit of sullen gloom or peevish irritability, during the continuance of which it was quite impossible for anyone to please him.

It was in this way that he revenged himself for his daughter's firm determination not to sacrifice herself to Clarke for the sake of restoring her father to the position which he coveted.

Without directly reproving her for this resolve, he showed by his manner that he was disappointed and offended with her for her refusal.

For example, at the breakfast table one morning, Mabel asked her father if she should not pass him the plate of biscuit.

He responded, with a deep sigh, "No, I have no appetite."

"Are you unwell?"

"I shall be soon if the mind has any effect upon the body," said Mr. Parker gloomily.

Mabel was silent, well knowing to what her father referred.

"I feel that this life is wearing upon me," he continued in a melancholy tone. "My temperament and my tastes unfit me for living in the wilderness. There is not a moment when the city and the old life I led there are out of my mind."

"Don't you think you would enjoy yourself better if you went about more?" asked Mabel. "There are some pleasant families about here."

"I have no spirits to go out," said Mr. Parker. "I should only carry gloom wherever I went."

"You think so now, father, but I think you would find your spirits imperceptibly rising."

"You know nothing about it, child. It may do for you who are young and can adapt yourself to new scenes, but for me it is impossible. I am like an old tree which has violently been torn up by the roots and removed to an uncongenial soil. As it will inevitably die, so I look forward to but a short time spent in wretchedness, after which Death will come as a happy release."

"Do not give yourself up to such gloomy fancies, father," said Mabel in deep distress. "You make me unhappy."

"I am sorry to blight your happiness," said Mr. Parker gloomily, "but it will only be for a short time. I shall pass away, and in the happiness of married life you will forget me."

"O, father, how can you talk so," remonstrated Mabel in deep concern.

"I do not speak this to reproach you," said Mr. Parker in the tone of a martyr. (It may be remarked that although he had declined to receive a biscuit when proffered by his daughter, he had helped himself and in spite of his despondency was eating with apparent relish.) "I do not say this to reproach you," he proceeded. "I suppose it is only natural that the young should be wholly wrapt up in themselves and their own plans, and so forget those who have passed before them on the stage of life. You are only like the rest. And perhaps it is all well. I have no desire to act as a kill-joy to your happiness, and though I am wretched myself, I have no disposition to interfere with your enjoyment of life."

"But how can I enjoy life when I see you so unhappy, father? Is there nothing I can do to restore you to cheerfulness?"

114

"There is but one thing," said her father, "and that is a thing which I shall not ask of you. If any sacrifice is to be made, it is best that I should make it. You have more years to live than I, and it is best that I should go to the grave rather than interfere with any of your plans."

This was setting the conduct of Mabel in an odious light, and, under the cover of resignation, really taxing her with selfishness and disregard to her father's happiness, while at the same time it undervalued the sacrifice which was demanded of her.

"Interfering with any of your plans" was certainly a mild way of expressing a marriage with one whom not only she did not like, but for whom she felt a positive repugnance.

"You mean that I can help you only by marrying Mr. Clarke," said Mabel with a troubled expression.

"That is the only way that will restore me to my former place in society and so prolong my life," said Mr. Parker. "But I am not so selfish as to require it at your hands. You would prefer to marry Henry Davenport and I do not wish to influence your choice. To one at my age, a few years more or less of life make little difference, and I freely confess that if, as it appears likely, my life is to be spent in this wilderness, I should prefer to die. Life can have no charms for me. It will, at least, be a consolation to me"—this was said in his gloomiest manner—"to feel that my daughter has nothing to interfere with her happiness."

As Mr. Parker said this, he supplied himself with his fourth biscuit, which he ate in a resigned way, as if he ate only because he felt that it was necessary to life.

All this was very trying to Mabel, who felt that all which her father said was meant as a reproach to her, particularly his references to her happiness.

"Father," she said, "I feel very much troubled by your unhappiness, and am sorry that I cannot do the only thing which would relieve you, but I cannot marry this Clarke. He is thoroughly odious to me. I feel a repugnance to him which I cannot account for."

"It is enough," said her father in a melancholy tone. "As I said, I do not wish to interfere with your plans, and if you prefer Henry Davenport—"

"Prefer!" repeated Mabel. "That is not the word. It would imply that this man Clarke was in any way tolerable."

"He is a lawyer in good standing," said her father severely. "Because you do not choose to marry him, you should not malign him."

Mabel was somewhat taken aback by this unexpected defense of the lawyer from her father's lips.

"At least you must admit his rascality in taking such an advantage of you as he is attempting to do."

"I am not clear about that," said Mr. Parker perversely. "All men are selfish—some more than others perhaps—but none are free from it. This man finds himself in possession of a secret which gives him the power of obtaining something which he is anxious to obtain. I do not know that we ought to blame him for availing himself of this for his own advantage."

"But, father, is it not dishonest to withhold that which belongs to another?" asked Mabel in considerable astonishment. "Would a man of honor adopt such a method of forcing a compliance with his desires?"

"As to honesty, Mabel, you will remember that he might have taken the money and said nothing about it to any of us. It is clear to me that whatever else may be said of him, he is not a mercenary man. No, he is evidently very much in love with you, and his love has led him to take advantage of this accidental discovery of the letter. No, I cannot permit you to speak of him unjustly, although it might be expected that I, upon whom his resolute persistence in standing by his condition falls heaviest,—it might be expected that I should be most disposed to reproach him. But though he has wronged me, I will yet be just to him."

"You are altogether too indulgent in your opinion of him," said Mabel.

"When you have lived to my age," said her father, "you

116

will learn to look upon the world with different eyes. There is not so much difference between different people as you may be tempted to believe. We all have a root of selfishness in us that goes down deeper than you may suppose. I have no doubt that this young lover of yours, Henry Davenport, would act in the same way as Mr. Clarke if he were placed in similar circumstances."

"You cannot mean so, father?" said Mabel with indignant emphasis. "Henry like this fellow Clarke! If I thought he would ever become so, I would never marry him!"

"I do not wish to lessen your confidence in him," said Mr. Parker, who by the way wished nothing more. "It is well that we should shut our eyes to the imperfections of our friends. Ignorance is the only bliss."

Mabel was about to remonstrate with her father for holding such low views of human nature when her attention was drawn to the figure of her lover as he dashed into the yard on horseback. Feeling convinced that something unusual brought him, and hoping that it might be to bring good tidings, she hastily rose from the table and went to the door to admit him.

Chapter XX.

A Consultation.

The joyful expression upon the face of her lover confirmed Mabel's anticipations.

Dismounting from his steed, he hastened to her side, saying, "Well, Mabel, what do you think I have got?"

"Not the letter!" she exclaimed eagerly. "You cannot have got the letter!"

"What do you call that, then?" he asked, triumphantly displaying the yellow and crumpled paper which was to them of such immense importance.

"Where did you get it?" asked Mabel breathlessly.

"I bought it!"

"Bought it?"

"Yes, and am to pay five hundred dollars for it."

"What can you mean, Henry?" asked the bewildered girl. "Surely the lawyer would not part with it for that sum."

"No, and probably he knows nothing of its disposal. The purchase was made of Zack."

"Of Zack?"

"Yes. I see you are surprised and will no longer keep you in suspense. You must know, then, that as I was riding in the forest I came upon our young hero apparently indulging in a fit of meditation. Accosting him, I inquired what occupied his thoughts, when he gradually led me on until he drew out our whole history, and ended by eliciting from me an offer of five hundred dollars for the missing letter, on which he at once produced the document and claimed the money. I feel so grateful to him for his thus removing the only impediment to our union that I shall faithfully keep my promise to him and pay him the money."

"I am more surprised than ever. How did Zack stumble upon such a valuable discovery?"

"He didn't appear able to give much information upon that point. He had been strolling along in the forest and accidentally came upon a pocket-book containing other papers, and among them, this."

"Belonging, of course, to the lawyer Clarke?"

"Yes, his name was upon it."

"Could he have dropped it?"

"Hardly, for it seemed to be empty so far as money is concerned. The probability is that it was stolen from him and the pocket-book and papers thrown away after the money had been taken. But there is Mehitable coming to the house in a high state of excitement apparently. What can have happened?"

Mehitable, it will be remembered, was just from the woods where she had accomplished the deliverance of the lawyer. It was altogether too remarkable an adventure for her to keep to herself, and she accordingly rushed into the presence of her young mistress in a fever of excitement, intent upon telling all that had befallen her.

"What is the matter, Mehitable?" asked Mabel in some curiosity. "I judge from your manner that something remarkable has occurred."

"So there has, Miss Mabel. Something *so* surprising, and to think that it should have been me that was the means of delivering him from his bonds."

"Him. Who do you mean by him?" asked Henry Davenport, with sudden interest, suspecting the truth.

"Why, Mr. Clarke, to be sure, the gentleman that is boarding to the tavern. O, he has such sweet, pretty manners."

"You seem to be quite in love with him, Mehitable."

"Me!" simpered Mehitable. "How can you talk so, Miss Mabel. And to be sure if I did it would not be surprising, for

119

he was so attentive. You can't think how polite and attentive he was. But I don't know whether it would be best to change my situation in life. Men are so deceitful!"

"Mehitable, I protest against this wholesale aspersion upon our sex," said Henry Davenport with mock indignation. "Fie upon you!"

"Perhaps I am wrong," said Mehitable, "but you know we girls have to be very circumspicious, don't we, Miss Mabel?"

"Certainly," responded Mabel, keeping her countenance with difficulty. "But you have not told us about Mr. Clarke. Did you say he was tied?"

"Yes, he was tied, hand and foot, and was laid under a tree. You can't think how my heart bled for him, Miss Mabel. I was walking along as innocent as could be, when all at once I heard a voice saying, 'Mehitable,' in gentle tones. I was flustrated, and going to run till I knew who it was. He asked me to untie the cords for him, and you can't think how happy I felt to think that it was I that came along just as I did. It would have been so dreadful if he had been obliged to stay there all night, and he might have caught cold, too."

Mabel and her lover exchanged a smile as they saw how deeply Mehitable had become interested in the lawyer.

"I suppose," said the young man jocosely, "that he repaid you with a kiss when you had freed him from his uncomfortable position."

Poor Mehitable! Her pride led her to think of using an evasion which might lead her auditors to imagine that she was admired by the object of her own admiration.

"If he did, I couldn't help it," she said modestly.

Young Davenport at first looked surprised, and then as he fathomed the spinster's motive, amused, but out of consideration for her feelings he did not imply any incredulity, though the lean, sallow, and wrinkled face of Mehitable certainly would warrant a doubt of her powers of fascination.

"How came Mr. Clarke in such a situation?" asked Mabel.

"It was all along of that wretch Indian John," said Mehitable. She added with energy, "If I could get hold of him I would scratch him."

"But what object could he have in binding Mr. Clarke? Did he have any grudge against him?"

"It wasn't that. It was because he was a thief. He wanted Mr. Clarke's money."

Here Mabel and young Davenport exchanged a look of intelligence. By questioning, they obtained from Mehitable all the additional information of which she was possessed. This however proved to be but slight.

A consultation was then held as to what was best to be done.

Of course, it occurred to them that the lawyer, finding his pocket-book gone, with its valuable papers missing, would feel uneasy and might be tempted to return to New York immediately and possess himself of the treasure before anyone else could make use of the information to be obtained from the paper.

This was by all means to be avoided. It would, therefore, be advisable to ease his mind by holding out some inducement of a disposition to yield to his solicitations and agree to a marriage, accompanied by the desire of more time for consideration.

It was decided not to communicate the discovery to Mr. Parker, lest by his changed manner he should awaken the lawyer's suspicions. Furthermore, it was arranged that Henry Davenport should at once proceed to New York and as quietly as possible remove the treasure to some other place, after which he would return and the marriage would take place.

This would probably occupy a fortnight, as in that day the means of communication between different parts of the country were in their infancy compared with the present day, and the distance of three hundred miles between there and New York could not well be traversed in much less than a week.

This arrangement was on many accounts decided to be the best that could be fixed upon, and Henry Davenport agreed to start for the city the very next day. Meanwhile, Mabel was to keep the lawyer in tow until it should no longer be necessary to fear him and enjoin Zack to say nothing whatever of what had occurred.

On the very next day, Clarke rode over to the Parkers'. Although he was well satisfied that the papers had been destroyed by the Indian, the bare possibility that the most valuable one might have been preserved made him feel somewhat uneasy, and he therefore wished to know how his prospects stood with Mabel.

To his gratified surprise she received him more gently than he had hoped. She told him frankly that her affections were set upon another and that it would be painful for her to part with him. Yet in a matter where her father's happiness seemed so much involved, she was not willing to decide hastily. She therefore begged him to allow her a fortnight in which to make up her mind.

Nothing in her manner excited the lawyer's suspicions and he left the house with a happy confidence that the campaign would close in fourteen days with the happiest results to him.

Meanwhile, Mehitable was weaving day-dreams—in which the lawyer and herself figured together. She even began to consider in what sort of a dress she should appear at the ceremony.

Chapter XXI.

Conclusion.

Young Davenport, spurred on by love and hope, made his way to New York with the utmost speed which that period admitted of. Yet the journey consumed three entire days. Now such are the improved facilities of locomotion that a few hours of easy riding would accomplish as much as the jolting of days.

On arriving at the city he made cautious inquiries as to the cottage occupied by Black Phoebe. It was located at the upper part of the island, so far above the then line of settlement that its value had been regarded as merely nominal. At the time of Mr. Parker's misfortunes, it had remained in his possession and, as before, he had continued to allow his child's old nurse to remain a free tenant. Upon the land connected with the house she raised a few vegetables, which together with a few little jobs which she found to do sufficed to yield her a comfortable support.

When Henry Davenport rode up, the old woman was at work just behind the house hoeing potatoes. She was still vigorous, although she could not have been less than eighty years of age. Although it was midsummer she wore a dress padded like a comforter of the present day. On her head she wore a white cloth which had been twisted into the form of a turban.

She looked up with curiosity, leaning on her hoe meanwhile, while the young man dismounted from his horse and, springing lightly over the fence, advanced towards her.

"How do you do this morning, Phoebe?" said Henry Davenport by way of salutation.

"Pretty comfortable," said the colored lady in a distant tone, scanning the young man's face critically. "I don't know you."

"But I hope you will, Aunt Phoebe, from this time forth. Who do you suppose has sent you a message by me?"

Phoebe shook her head.

"Then you can't tell?"

"There ain't nobody that would take the trouble to send a message to old Phoebe, except it may be that beloved child Mabel, and she's gone away off into the woods among the wild Indians. Oh my, it seems, sometimes, as if I couldn't go to the kingdom without seeing that ar blessed child once again."

"I saw her only three or four days since, Aunt Phoebe," said the young man.

"You saw the dear child Mabel?" asked Phoebe, dropping her hoe in joyful surprise. "And did she send any message to her Aunt Phoebe?"

"She sent her love to Aunt Phoebe, and thinks she shall come to see her before long."

"Bless her dear heart! It will be a joyful day for old Phoebe. And when will she come?"

"As soon as she is married, Aunt Phoebe," said Henry with a smile.

"Married!" exclaimed Aunt Phoebe, holding up both hands in astonishment. "That baby going to be married!"

"But she isn't a baby now, Aunt Phoebe! She's a grown up young lady!"

"She'll always be a baby to me," said the old nurse. "Don't I remember how often I have carried the dear child in these arms and pillowed her head on my bosom? O law, them were happy times. It don't seem as if she could be old enough to be married. And who is going to marry the dear baby?"

"It is a young man named Davenport."

"It's a good name," said Phoebe. "I knowed a Davenport family once, but they went back to England. And is this young man a good man, and will he be good to the dear child?"

"That he will I am sure, Aunt Phoebe. He loves her very much."

"I am glad of that. I am glad of that. And how does he look? Is he handsome?"

"Why, as to that, Aunt Phoebe, I'll leave you to judge for yourself," said the young man blushing.

"Are you the one that is to marry Mabel?" said the old woman earnestly.

"Yes, Aunt Phoebe."

Phoebe came forward, and resting her hand hard and shrivelled by age and toil upon the young man's shoulder, looked long and earnestly in his face. She was striving to discern by the outward expression the soul that lay behind and to judge whether he was worthy of her pet child. It was touching to see the anxious concern of the old nurse for the welfare of her favorite—the affection which nothing could abate which drew her to the child that had nestled in her bosom.

The scrutiny, which was a long one, apparently resulted favorably, for Phoebe, drawing a long breath of relief, said, "I know you will be kind and loving to the dear child. There's something in your face that tells me so. And will you some time bring her to see old Phoebe?"

"That I will, Aunt Phoebe. Probably before a month is over, we shall come to New York for a short time, and perhaps Mr. Parker will come here to live. But that will depend upon circumstances that I am about to tell you. Knowing your interest in the family, I am about to tell you a secret, Aunt Phoebe."

Nothing could have pleased Aunt Phoebe better than this promise, not alone because she possessed a fair share of that curiosity which is said to be a characteristic trait of her sex, but also because she was proud of the confidence which such a disclosure evinced.

It is unnecessary to follow Henry Davenport in his

relation of the circumstances under which the treasure was concealed. It will be remembered that in the letter of the late Mr. Parker it was stated that the money had been buried in the temporary absence of Phoebe, to whom it had been thought wisest not to divulge it, not from any doubts as to her fidelity but because it would have done no good to make the disclosure. Now, however, Henry Davenport thought best to make a confidant of her, because any other course would be beset by embarrassments, and Phoebe might be of essential service to him in assisting him to unearth the treasure and conceal it in her cottage until it could be disposed of in some other way.

As may well be imagined, she listened to the story with the greatest show of wonder and interrupted the speaker several times by ejaculations expressive of her surprise.

"Under dat ar apple tree!" she exclaimed. "And to think I've been here so many years and never thought there was so much treasure just under my feet. O law! what a strange world it is, anyhow."

But when, in the course of the narrative, young Davenport came to speak of the manner in which Clarke the lawyer attempted to secure his own interests her indignation became intense.

"*He* wanted to marry my baby?" she exclaimed in scorn. "He ain't good enough to marry old Phoebe, much less that dear blessed angel Mabel. O, I wish he'd come here. I only wish he'd come just once. Dat's all I'd ask. I'd—"

Here Phoebe brandished her hoe with an air of decided menace which told expressively enough what sort of a reception the lawyer would have been likely to receive at the hands of the faithful old nurse.

Henry Davenport smiled at her enthusiasm which he shared in her feelings towards the lawyer.

It was determined at once to proceed to digging for the treasure. As there were no houses nearby, and it was not in sight from the road, this step was not considered imprudent. Stripping off his coat, Henry Davenport proceeded to dig with energy. Notwithstanding his confidence, he could not help feeling his heart beat a little faster as he approached the realization of his hopes. At length the spade struck a hard substance.

"Dat's it!" exclaimed Phoebe, clasping his arm. "O, for de love of Heaven, child, work as quick as you can."

Finding that he was on the track, Henry began to dig with greater energy than before and at length revealed the top of a chest, very strongly resembling those now used by sailors. Digging around it he discovered that it was securely tied by ropes.

"Quick, Aunt Phoebe! haven't you scissors that I can cut these cords with?"

Phoebe hobbled into the cottage and brought out a huge jack-knife, black and rusty, which looked as if it might have shared a laborious life.

"Dat knife was guv me by old Mr. Parker fifty years ago," said she in a tone of reminiscence. But Henry Davenport was in no mood to hear reminiscences. Snatching the knife from the hands of his sable companion, he applied the blade to the rope and succeeded by dint of considerable exertion in severing it. A moment afterwards, and the lid, thrown back, disclosed the glittering, golden contents of the old chest.

The Hidden Treasure lay revealed!

"Who'd a thought it?" exclaimed Phoebe, throwing up her hands in amazement. "O de Lor' if I'd a knowed all dat gold was so nearby, I shouldn't a slept nights, thinking of the robbers and bugglers. I should sartainly have expected to wake up some morning and find my throat cut."

"Do you think you'd have waked up under those circumstances?" queried Henry quizically.

Leaving the two to dispose of the discovered treasure as prudence dictated, we go back to Mr. Parker's family.

Mr. Parker, unaware of the favorable change which had taken place in his circumstances, was still nervous and irritable. Mabel, sustained by hope, bore all with unruffled serenity. As for Clarke, he felt that matters were approaching a crisis. The gold which Indian John had stolen from him constituted the bulk of what he had on hand, so that by the end of a fortnight he would have barely enough left to carry him back to the city. But he did not suffer this to trouble him much, feeling assured that Mabel would finally yield. Knowing very well that this would not be from any preference for him personally, he thought it wisest to keep out of her way and employed his time in hunting and fishing.

At length the fortnight expired.

With a heart elate with hope, Clarke rode over to the residence of his prospective father-in-law.

When he was admitted into the sitting-room, Mabel and her father were present. On the night previous Henry Davenport had arrived, bringing a portion of the gold and a certificate of deposit of the rest in one of the city banks. Then, for the first time, Mr. Parker was told of what had occurred. The effect was to transport him into the seventh heaven of happiness.

The lawyer had not heard of the young man's arrival. Indeed, although he knew of his absence, he did not know where he had been.

Clarke advanced into the room with an air of easy indifference and affably bade Mabel and her father good morning.

"I'm a man of business, Mr. Parker," he said, rubbing his hands, "and so are you. Let me hope that you and your charming daughter have considered favorably the proposal I have made and are prepared to accept it."

"In that case," said Mabel, "you are prepared, of course, to give up to my father the letter of which you came into possession?"

The lawyer looked slightly embarrassed.

"I haven't it with me," he said, "just at this moment."

"Doubtless you have it at the tavern, then. You must pardon us for being over-careful, but the circumstances seem to justify it."

The lawyer paused a moment in embarrassment.

"To tell the truth," he said, "I did not bring the letter with me on this journey. I thought there would be considerable risk in losing it and accordingly left it in New York at my office."

"How are we to know that we have such a letter, then?" asked Mr. Parker.

"On my word of honor as a gentleman—" commenced the lawyer.

"I am sorry you esteem your word so lightly," said Mabel coolly.

As she spoke she took from the table a letter which Clarke at once recognized at the one which he had lost.

"Confusion!" he muttered, while his heart sank within him.

A moment afterwards his confidence returned. They now were made acquainted with the repository of the hidden treasure, but so was he also. By hastening to New York he might anticipate them yet and get possession of the gold.

As this thought struck him, he turned to leave the room. But Mabel had read his thought and interrupted his departure by saying, "Perhaps it will save you some trouble, Mr. Clarke, if I say that this letter has been in our possession a fortnight and during that time Mr. Davenport has been to New York. He returned last night."

The lawyer understood that his game was up and cursed himself for his folly in not going as soon as he met with his loss. Now all was lost!

As he left the house—it might have been chance—he fell in with Mehitable. In the course of a conversation which ensued he learned that that young lady was the possessor of five hundred dollars which she had partly inherited and partly laid up. His affairs were so involved that he was ready for anything, and before the twain separated the delighted Mehitable had received an offer which she promptly accepted. The pair at once proceeded to the village where they were united by an accommodating justice.

129

Two hours after, in the midst of many speculations as to the cause of her absence (for it was approaching dinner-time) Mehitable appeared.

"What could induce you to leave me for so long, Mehitable?" asked Mabel reproachfully.

"You will please address me by my proper name," said Mehitable bridling.

"Miss Higgins perhaps?" said Mabel, somewhat amused.

"I am no longer Miss Higgins," said Mehitable loftily. "I am a married woman."

"Is the woman crazy?" ejaculated Mabel in astonishment.

"No, Miss Parker," said Mehitable proudly. "You will please address me as Mrs. Clarke from this time. I came to say that I am boarding with my husband at the tavern and shall not be able to assist you in your domestic duties any more. I will send over for my trunk and bandbox tomorrow."

"Crackey, who'd have thought Mehitable would ever have got married!" exclaimed Zack, who had come up in time to hear the announcement. "Well, I guess nobody need be afraid of being an old maid now."

"I scorn your insinuations, Zachariah," said Mehitable, tossing her head.

"Won't you send me some of the wedding-cake?" asked Zack demurely.

It may be said here that after a few months of married life Clarke deserted his fair bride, having previously contrived to make away with all her small hoard. The loss was, however, made up to her by Mabel, and she still lives in the village, clinging to the name of Mrs. Clarke despite the unworthiness of the man through whom she obtained it. She bears her loss with fortitude and evidently esteems his name as better than his company.

According to the arrangement already intimated, Mr. Parker took up his residence in the city where he enjoys life in the company of his old acquaintances, whose remembrance returned as soon as it was ascertained that he was again in good circumstances. Mabel and her husband visited the city in the winter, but passed their summers in the beautiful spot where they first met and loved. Mrs. Mehitable Clarke presided over their establishment during their absence and found a home there during the year.

As for Zack, in whom it is hoped the reader has not been wholly uninterested, he became more studious as he grew older and has since risen to distinction at the bar. His wild, boyish spirits, toned down in maturer years, rendered him a delightful companion and a universal favorite.

Black Phoebe lived long enough to see Mabel happily married and to trot a younger Mabel upon her knees. She died full of age, and tears of grateful remembrance were shed over her grave by the object of her love.

I must not close this chronicle without speaking of our Indian friends. The village of Okommakamesit is no more. The ruthless march of European civilization has swept over it, and a factory stands on the former site of Long Arrow's lodge. But far beyond the Mississippi, Okanoga and Waurega still live at a good old age, surrounded by children and grandchildren who see that the wigwam of the old couple is well supplied with venison and corn. Their lives have been tranquil and happy and now with joyful anticipation they look forward to the summons that shall open to them the happy hunting grounds, to which Long Arrow has long preceded them.